"What? Did you forget to frisk me before I leave the building?"

"Don't tempt me, Sally," Kirk said.

"Don't be so pompous. You've lied to me from the moment you met me. Why not try being honest for a change?"

"You want honest? I'll give you honest. You caught my eye the second you arrived in the bar that night. I didn't recognize you immediately but I couldn't take my eyes off you."

She snorted. "I may be naive, but don't expect me to believe that. There were any number of women far more beautiful than me in the bar that night."

"And yet I only had eyes for you."

The look she gave him was skeptical. "A little clichéd, wouldn't you say?"

"Stop trying to put up walls between us." Kirk stepped forward and took her by the arm. "You're still carrying my baby," he said. "I have a duty to care for...my child."

He wasn't holding her firmly, but he wasn't letting go, either. It drove home the fact that the life she thought she'd had was not her own.

* * *

Little Secrets: The Baby Merger is part of the Little Secrets series: Untamed passion, unexpected pregnancy...

Dear Reader,

Every now and then I have been lucky enough to visit the beautiful city of Seattle in the course of my husband's work. It's a city I've grown to love and it genuinely feels like a home away from home for me now. In fact, I wish I could visit more often and get to know the city and the whole of Washington State a great deal better. It felt only natural to set this story in the Emerald City. Any mistakes in setting are very much my own.

After briefly meeting Sally in a previous book I'd written (*Arranged Marriage, Bedroom Secrets*) I felt she needed her own happy ever after and in *Little Secrets: The Baby Merger*, Sally is determined to prove to her father she is intelligent and worthy of standing at his side in business. But her father's appointment of a new VP shows her exactly what he thinks of her and her abilities. When an attempt to drown her sorrows leads to an uncharacteristic one-night stand with a handsome stranger, the last thing Sally expects to find is that she's pregnant...by her new boss!

For Kirk Tanner, Sally's pregnancy is an unexpected wrench in the works, especially since he suspects she may be responsible for the leaks that could lead to a hostile takeover of the company.

I do hope you'll love reading *Little Secrets: The Baby Merger*. Feel free to drop me a line via my website, www.yvonnelindsay.com, or visit my Facebook page, www.Facebook.com/yvonnelindsayauthor.

Happy reading!

Yvonne Lindsay

YVONNE LINDSAY

—

LITTLE SECRETS: THE BABY MERGER

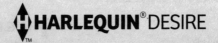

Recycling programs
for this product may
not exist in your area.

ISBN-13: 978-0-373-83870-7

Little Secrets: The Baby Merger

Copyright © 2017 by Dolce Vita Trust

Printed in U.S.A.

www.Harlequin.com

A typical Piscean, *USA TODAY* bestselling author **Yvonne Lindsay** has always preferred her imagination to the real world. Married to her blind-date hero and with two adult children, she spends her days crafting the stories of her heart, and in her spare time she can be found with her nose in a book reliving the power of love, or knitting socks and daydreaming. Contact her via her website, yvonnelindsay.com.

Books by Yvonne Lindsay

Harlequin Desire

The Wife He Couldn't Forget
Lone Star Holiday Proposal
One Heir...or Two?

Wed at Any Price

Honor-Bound Groom
Stand-In Bride's Seduction
For the Sake of the Secret Child

Courtesan Brides

Arranged Marriage, Bedroom Secrets
Contract Wedding, Expectant Bride

Little Secrets

Little Secrets: The Baby Merger

Visit her Author Profile page at Harlequin.com, or yvonnelindsay.com, for more titles.

This one is dedicated to my family,
each of whom hold a piece of my heart
in their hands and whose love and support
keep me going every day.

One

A flash of pale gold hair near the entrance caught Kirk's attention in the dimness of the bar. A woman came through the door, a tall, well-built man close behind her. She turned and said something, and the muscle looked like he was going to object, but then she spoke again—gesturing vaguely across the room—and he nodded and disappeared outside. Interesting, Kirk thought. Clearly the guy was an employee of some kind, perhaps a bodyguard, and he'd obviously been dismissed.

Kirk took a sip of his beer and watched the woman move through the area, searching for someone. There was an unconscious sensuality to the way she moved. Dressed down in a pair of slim-fitting trousers topped by a long-sleeved, loose tunic, she seemed to be trying to hide her tempting mix of curves and slenderness, but he saw enough to pique his interest. Most women hated it when they had well-rounded hips and a decent butt, and judging by the way she'd dressed to conceal, she was one of those women who wasn't a fan of her shape and form. But he was. In fact, he really liked her shape and form.

Who was she meeting here? A partner, he wondered, feeling a small prick of envy as his eyes skimmed her from head to foot. The weariness that had driven him here tonight in search of better company than employee files and financial forecasts slid away in increments as his eyes appreciatively roamed her body.

He knew the instant she saw the person she was looking for. Her features lit up, and she raised a hand in greeting, moving more quickly now toward her target. Kirk scanned ahead of her, feeling himself relax when he saw the couple who reached out to greet her affectionately. Not a partner, then, he thought with a smile and took a sip of the malty craft beer he'd ordered earlier.

He noticed one of her friends pass her a martini and pondered on the fact that they'd already ordered her drink for her. Obviously she was a reliable type, both punctual and predictable. Too bad those were not the traits of someone who might be interested in a short, intense fling, which was all he was in the market for. He had his life plan very firmly set out in front of him, and while his company's merger with Harrison Information Technology here in Bellevue,

Washington, would definitely fast-track things, a committed relationship was still not in the cards for a long time. When he was ready, he'd tackle that step the way he did everything else, with a lot of research and dedication to getting it right the first time. Kirk Tanner did not make mistakes—and he definitely wasn't looking for love.

Kirk turned his attention away from the woman, but something about her kept tickling at the back of his mind. Something familiar that he couldn't quite place. He looked across the room and studied her more closely, noting again the swath of pale gold hair that fell over her shoulders and just past her shoulder blades. Even from here he could see the kinks in her hair that told him she'd recently had it tied up in a tight ponytail. His fingers clenched around his glass, suddenly itching to push through the length of it, to see if it felt as silky soft as it looked.

As if she sensed his regard, the woman turned and glanced past him before returning her attention to her friends. This gave him the most direct view so far of her face—and yes, there was definitely something familiar about her. He'd certainly have remembered if he'd met her before but perhaps he'd seen her photograph somewhere.

Kirk searched his eidetic memory. Ah, yes, now he had it—Sally Harrison, the only child of Orson Harrison, the chairman of Harrison Information Technology. The very firm his own company was officially merging with at 3:00 p.m. tomorrow. The idea of a merger with Sally Harrison held distinct appeal, even though he knew she should be strictly off-limits.

Her personnel file had intrigued him, although the head shot attached to it had hardly done her justice. He scoured his memory for more details. Since high school she'd interned in every department of the head office of HIT. In fact, she probably knew more about how each sector of the company ran than her father did, and that was saying something. She'd graduated from MIT with a PhD in social and engineering systems. And yet, despite her experience and education and the fact she was the chairman's daughter, she'd apparently never aspired to anything higher than a mediocre middle-management position.

Granted, her department was a high performer and several of her staff had been promoted, but why hadn't she moved ahead, too? Was she being very deliberately kept in place by her father or other senior staff? Was there something not noted in her file that made her unqualified or ill-suited for a more prominent position in the company?

And—the more compelling question—did she perhaps have sour grapes about her lack of advancement?

Her knowledge about the firm made her a prime candidate for the investigation her father had asked him to undertake as part of his staff evaluation during the merger.

Under the guise of seeing where staff cutbacks needed to be made, he was also tasked with investigating who could most likely be responsible for what could be unwitting or deliberate leaks to HIT's largest business rival. Orson suspected that the rival company, DuBecTec, was accumulating data to undermine his company with a view toward making a hostile takeover bid in the next few months. He had instructed Kirk to look at everyone on the payroll very thoroughly. Everyone including the very appealing Ms. Sally Harrison.

Kirk took another sip of his beer and watched her across the room. She'd barely sipped her drink yet but swirled the toothpick in her martini around and around. Just then, as he was watching, she removed the toothpick from her drink and, using her teeth and her tongue, drew the cocktail onion off the tip and crunched down. His entire body clenched on a surge of desire so intense he almost groaned out loud.

Sally Harrison was a very interesting subject indeed, he decided as he willed his body back under control. And before he left the bar tonight, he would definitely find a way to get to know her better.

Company merger. For the best.

Even though she was going through the motions, saying all the right things as her friends excitedly told her about their recent honeymoon, Sally couldn't stop thinking about her father's shocking announcement over dinner tonight. If she hadn't heard it straight from the horse's mouth, she would have struggled to believe it. She *still* struggled to believe it. And the fact that her father hadn't shared a moment of what had to have been an extensive forerunner to the merger with her raked across her emotions.

It was a harsh reminder that if she was the kind of person who actually stood *with* her father, versus sheltering behind him, she'd have been a part of the discussions. Not only that, if she'd been the kind of person she ought to be, confident and charismatic instead of shy and intense, this entire merger might not even have been necessary.

Her whole body trembled with a sense of failure. Oh, sure, logically she knew that her dad wouldn't have entered into this planned merger if it wasn't the best thing for Harrison IT and its thousand or so staff worldwide. And it wasn't as though he needed her input. As chairman of HIT, he held the reins very firmly in both hands, as he always had. But, until now, HIT had been the family firm, and darn it, she was his family. Or at least she was the last time she'd looked.

Of course, now the company would be rebranded—Harrison Tanner Tech. Clearly things were about to change on more than one level.

She could have predicted her father's response when she'd questioned the secrecy surrounding the merger.

"Nothing you need to worry about," he'd said, brushing her off in his usual brusque but loving way.

And she wasn't worried—not about the company, anyway. But she did have questions that he'd been very evasive about answering. Like, why this *particular* other company? What did it bring to HIT that the firm didn't have already? Why *this* man, whoever he was, who was being appointed vice president effective tomorrow? And why did her dad want her to be there during the video link when he and the new vice president of the newly branded Harrison Tanner Tech would make the merger announcement simultaneously to the whole staff? She couldn't think of anything she'd rather do less. Aside from the fact that she hated being in the public arena, how on earth would she look her colleagues in the eye afterward and possibly have to face their accusations that she'd known about this merger all along? Or worse, have to admit that she hadn't. Just the thought of it made her stomach flip uneasily.

Her father had always told her he worked hard so she didn't have to. She knew he worked hard. Too hard, if the recent tired and gray cast to his craggy features was anything to go by. It was another prod that she hadn't pulled her weight. Hadn't been the support he deserved and maybe even needed. Not that he'd ever say as much. He'd protected her all her life, which hadn't abated as she'd reached adulthood. To her shame, she'd let him.

Thing was, she *wanted* to work hard. She wanted to be a valued member of HIT and to be involved in the decision making. She wished she could shed the anxiety that led to her always hovering in the shadows and allowing others to run with her ideas and get the glory that came with those successes. Okay, so not every idea was wildly successful, but her phobia of speaking in groups had held her back, and she knew others had been promoted over her because of it. Her personality flaws meant she wasn't perceived to be as dynamic and forward thinking as people in upper management were expected to be.

When her crippling fear had surfaced after the death of her mom, and when years of therapy appeared to make no headway, her father had always reassured her that she was simply a late bloomer and she only needed time to come into her own. But she was twenty-eight now, and she still hadn't overcome her insecurities. She knew that was a continual, if quiet, disappointment to her father. While he'd never said as much, she knew he'd always hoped that she could overcome her phobia and stand at his side at HIT, and she'd wanted that, too. She'd thought he was still giving her time. She hadn't realized he'd given up on her. Not until today.

This latest development was the last straw. Her father had always included her in his planning for the firm, even implemented an idea or two of hers from time to time, but this he'd done completely without her.

The shock continued to reverberate through her. The writing was on the wall. She'd been left in the dark on this major decision—and in the dark was where she'd stay going forward unless she did something about it. She couldn't make excuses for herself anymore. She was a big girl now. It was past time that she stretched to her full potential. If she didn't, she'd be overlooked for the rest of her life, and she knew for sure that she didn't want that. Things had to change. She had to change. Now.

Gilda and Ron were still laughing and talking,

sharing reminiscences as well as exchanging those little touches and private looks that close couples did all the time. It was sweet, but it compounded the sense of exclusion she felt at the same time. In her personal life as well as in the workplace, the people around her seemed to move forward easily, effortlessly, while she struggled with every step. She was happy for the others, truly—she was just sad for herself.

When they both looked at their watches and said they needed to be on their way, she didn't object. Instead she waved them off with a smile and stayed to finish her barely touched drink.

She should go home to her apartment, get an early night—prepare for the big announcement tomorrow. Should? It felt like all her life Sally had done what *should* be done. Like she'd spent her life striving to please others. But what about her? Change had to start from a point in time—why couldn't that change start now? Why couldn't she be bold? Accept new challenges?

"Ma'am? The gentleman over there asked me to bring you this."

A waitress put another Gibson on the table in front of her. Sally blinked in surprise before looking up at the girl.

"Gentleman?"

"Over there." The waitress gestured. "He's really hot."

"Are you sure it was for me?" she asked.

"He was quite specific. Did you want me to take it back?"

Did she? The frightened mouse inside her quivered and said, *oh, yes.* But wasn't that what she would have done normally? In fact, since she'd dismissed her personal security, wouldn't she normally have left with Gilda and Ron and shared a cab so she wouldn't be left on her own like this? Open to new experiences? Meeting new people? Flirting with a man?

Sally turned her head and met the gaze of the man in question. She'd noticed him before and rejected him as being way out of her league. *Hot* didn't even begin to describe him. He wore confidence as easily as he wore his dark suit and crisp, pale business shirt, top button undone. Sally felt every cell in her body jump to visceral attention as his eyes met hers. He nodded toward her, raised his glass in a silent toast, then smiled. The kind of smile that sizzled to the ends of her toes.

Be bold, a little voice whispered in the back of her mind. She turned her attention to the waitress and gave the girl a smile.

"Ma'am?"

"Leave it. Thank you. And please pass on my thanks."

"Oh, you can do that yourself. He's coming over."

Coming over? Sally's fight-or-flight reflexes asserted themselves in full screaming glory, shrieking, *take flight!* like a Klaxon blaring in the background.

"May I join you?" the man said smoothly, his hand hovering over the back of the chair Gilda had recently vacated.

"Certainly." Her pulse fluttered at her throat, but she managed to sound reasonably calm. She lifted her glass and tipped it toward him in a brief toast. "Thank you for the drink."

"You're welcome. You don't see many people drinking a Gibson these days. An old-fashioned drink for an old-fashioned girl?"

His voice was rich and deep and stroked her nerves like plush velvet on bare skin. And he certainly wasn't hard on the eyes, either. He filled his suit with broad shoulders, and the fine cotton of his shirt stretched across a chest that looked as though it had the kinds of peaks and valleys of toned muscle that a woman like her appreciated but oh so rarely got to indulge in. His face was slightly angular, his nose a straight blade, and his eyes—whatever color they were, something light, but it was hard to tell in here—looked directly at her. No shrinking violet, then. Not like her. His lips were gently curved. He didn't have the look of a man who smiled easily, and yet his smile didn't look fake. In fact, he actually looked genuinely amused but not in a superior way.

Not quite sure how to react, she looked down at her drink and forced a smile. "Something like that."

Sally looked up again in time to see him grin outright in response. Seeing his smile was like receiving an electric shock straight to her girlie parts. Wow. Shouldn't a man need a license to wield that much sex appeal?

"I'm Kirk, and you are?" He offered her his hand and quirked an eyebrow at her.

Sally's insides turned to molten liquid. Normally, she wouldn't give in to a drink and a slick delivery like the one he'd just pitched, but what the hell. She was fed up with being the good girl. The one who always did what was expected. The one who always deferred to others and never put herself forward or chased after what she wanted. If she wanted to make a stand in anything in her life, she was going to have to do things head-on rather than work quietly and happily in the background. Hadn't she just decided tonight to take charge of her life and her decisions? For once, she was going to do exactly what she wanted and damn the consequences.

She put out her hand to accept his. "I'm Sally. Next round is on me."

"Good to meet you, although I have to warn you, I don't usually let women buy me drinks."

Sally felt that old familiar clench in her gut when faced with conflict. The kind of thing that made her clam up, afraid to speak up for herself. It was one of her major failings—another thing she hid behind. But she'd told herself she wouldn't hide tonight. She pasted a stiff smile on her lips. Pushed herself to respond.

"Oh, really? Why is that?"

"I'm kind of old-fashioned, too."

She couldn't stifle the groan that escaped her. Despite being head of a leading IT corporation, her dad was also the epitome of old-fashioned. The very last thing Sally needed in her life was another man like that.

"But," he continued, still smiling, "in your case I might be prepared to make an exception."

Taken aback, she blurted, "In my case? Why?"

"Because I don't think you're just buying me a drink just so you can take advantage of my body."

She couldn't help it. She laughed out loud. Not a pretty, dainty little titter—a full-blown belly laugh.

"Does that happen often?" she asked.

"Now and again," he admitted.

"Trust me, you're quite safe with me," she reassured him.

"Really?"

Was it her imagination, or did he sound a little disappointed?

"Well, perhaps we should wait and see," she answered with a smile of her own and reached for her martini.

Two

How had it gone from a few drinks and dancing to this? Sally asked herself as they entered his apartment. Kirk threw his jacket over the back of a bland beige sofa. She got only the vaguest impression of his place—a generic replica of so many serviced apartments used by traveling business people with stock-standard wall decorations and furnishings. The only visible sign of human occupation was the dining table piled high with archive boxes and files.

That was all she noticed before his hands were lifting her hair from her nape and his lips pressed just there. She shivered at the contact. Kirk let her hair drop again and took her hand to lead her through to his bedroom. He turned to face her, and she trembled at the naked hunger reflected in his eyes.

Be bold, Sally reminded herself. *You wanted this. Take charge. Take what you want.*

She reached for his tie, pulling it loose, sliding it out from under his collar and letting it drop to the floor. Then she attacked his buttons, amazed that her fingers still had any dexterity at all given how her body all but vibrated with the fierceness of her longing for this man. A piece of her urged her to slow down, to take care, to reconsider, but she relegated that unwelcome advice to the very back of her mind. This was what she wanted, and she would darn well take it, and him, and revel in the process.

Kirk didn't remain passive. His large, warm hands stroked her through the fabric of her tunic, which, beneath his touch, felt like the sexiest thing she'd ever worn. She sighed out loud when she pushed his shirt free of his body and skimmed her hands over the breadth of his muscled shoulders, following the contours of his chest. While they'd danced, she'd been able to tell he was in shape, but, wow, this guy was *really* in shape. For a second she felt uncomfortable, ashamed of her own inadequacies—her small breasts, her wide hips, her heavy bottom. But then Kirk bent his head and nuzzled at the curve of her neck, and the sensation of his hot breath and his lips against her skin consigned all rational thought to obscurity.

For now everything was about his touch. She was vaguely aware of Kirk reaching for the zipper at the back of her tunic and sliding it down, then deftly removing her trousers, and felt again that prickle of insecurity as he eased the garment off her body, exposing her pretty lace bra and her all too practical full briefs.

She stifled a giggle. "Sorry, I wasn't quite expecting this outcome when I dressed for today."

"Never apologize," he ordered. His voice was deep and held a tiny tremor, which gave her an immense boost of confidence. "You're beautiful. Perfect, in fact. And, for the record, I happen to find white cotton incredibly sexy."

She looked at his face—studying it to see if he was serious or if he was simply saying what he thought she needed to hear—but there was an honesty there in his features that sent a new thrill through her. She bracketed his cheeks with her hands and pulled his face down to hers, kissing him with all that she had in her. With just a few well-chosen words, he'd made her feel valued, whether he knew it or not.

She couldn't pinpoint the exact moment he unhooked her bra, but she would remember forever the first time his hands cupped her breasts. His touch was reverent but firm. His fingers, when they caressed her nipples, teasing but gentle. Unable to help herself, Sally arched her back, pressing herself against his palms, eager to feel more. She was no shrinking virgin, but she'd never experienced this kind of responsiveness before in her life. Right now she was lost in sensation and anticipation of his next move.

When he lowered his mouth to capture one taut nipple, she keened softly in response. Her legs felt like jelly, as if they could barely support her, and at her core her body had developed a deep, drawing ache of need.

"Perfect," he whispered against her wet and sensitive bud, sending another shiver through her body that had nothing to do with cold and everything to do with an inferno of heat and desire.

Kirk's hands were at her hips a moment later, easing her panties down over her thighs. She stepped out of them, for the first time in her adult life unembarrassed by her nakedness.

"It seems you have me at a slight disadvantage here," she said with a teasing smile.

"I'm all for equal opportunity." He smiled in return and spread his hands wide so she could reach for his belt buckle.

She wasn't sure how he did it, but he managed to make shedding his shoes, socks, trousers and boxer briefs incredibly sexy. Or maybe it was just that she was so looking forward to seeing him naked, to having the opportunity to investigate every curve of muscle and every shadow beneath it, that every new inch of bared skin aroused her even more.

His skin peppered with goose bumps as she trailed her hand from his chest to his lower abdomen. His erection was full and heavy, jutting proudly from his body without apology or shame.

"You do that to me," he said as she eyed him.

Again he made her feel as though she was the strong, desirable one here. The one with all the authority and control. Without a second thought, she wrapped her fingers around his length, stroking him and marveling at the contradiction in impressions— of the heated satin softness of his skin and the steel-like hardness beneath it.

Somehow they maneuvered onto the bed. Again an exercise in elegance rather than the convoluted tangle of limbs she'd always experienced in the past. Sally had never known such synchronicity before. Exploring his body, listening to and watching his re-actions as she did so, became the most natural thing in the world. Despite the sense of urgency that had gripped her at the bar, right now she wanted to take all the time in the world. Kirk, too, seemed content to go along for the ride, to allow her the time to find out exactly what wrung the greatest reactions from him, how to take him to the edge of madness and how to bring him slowly down again.

And then it was his turn. His hands were firm and sure as they stroked her, his fingers nimble and sweet as they tweaked and tugged and probed until she was shaking from head to foot. Wanting to de-mand he give her the release her body trembled for, yet wanting him to prolong this torturous pleasure at the same time. And all the while he murmured how beautiful she was. How perfect. It was the most em-powering experience of her life.

When he finally sheathed himself and entered her body, it was sheer perfection. Her hips rose to greet him, and as he filled her she knew she'd never known anything quite this exquisite and might never know anything to match it again. Tonight was a gift.

Something to be cherished. All of it—especially the way he made her feel so incredibly wanted when he groaned and gripped her hips as he sank fully within her.

"Don't. Move," he implored her as she tightened her inner muscles around him.

"What? Like this?" She tightened again and tilted her hips so he nestled just that little bit deeper.

"Exactly *not* like that."

She did it again, savoring the power his words had given her. Savoring, too, each and every sensation that rippled through her body at how deliciously he filled her. He growled, a deep, guttural resignation to her demands and began to withdraw. Then he surged against her. This time it was Sally who groaned in surrender. Her hands tightened on his shoulders, her short, practical nails embedded in his skin. She met him thrust for thrust, her tension coiling tighter and tighter, until she lost all sense of what was happening and felt her entire being let go in a maelstrom of pleasure so mind-blowing, so breathtaking she knew nothing in her life would ever be the same again.

As she lay there, heart still hammering a frantic beat, her nerve endings still tingling with the climax that had wrung her body out, she thought it such a shame that this was to be only a one-night stand. A woman could get used to this kind of lovemaking. But not a woman like her, she reminded herself sternly. She had a career path to follow. A life to build and a point to prove, to herself if to no one else. Throwing herself into another doomed attempt at building a satisfying relationship would only distract her from her goals. She had to take this rendezvous for what it was—a beautiful anomaly—and then thank the nice man for the lovely ending to the night before getting dressed and going home.

She couldn't quite bring herself to do it. To pull away and leave the welcoming warmth of his embrace, to end the age-old connection of their bodies. Kirk murmured something in her ear and rolled to one side, bringing her with him until she was half sprawled over his body. Oh, but he was magnificent, she though as she studied his upper torso. How lucky was she to have met him tonight? She lowered her head on his chest and listened to his heart rate as it changed from racing fast to a slower, more even beat. His breathing, too, changed, and his fingers stopped playing with her hair.

He was asleep. Five more minutes and it was time to go. Gently she extracted herself from his arms and tiptoed around the bedroom gathering up her things. A quick trip to the bathroom to tidy up and get dressed and she was out of here. No sticking around for embarrassment in the cold light of morning. No recriminations or awkwardness over breakfast.

She let herself out of the apartment and slipped her phone from her bag. She'd just opened an app to order a cab when her phone—put on silent when she'd gone out to meet her friends—lit up with an incoming call. She recognized the name on the screen immediately. Marilyn had been her father's PA since before she was born and had become a mother figure to Sally after her own mother's death. But it was late, after midnight. What on earth was Marilyn doing calling her now?

"Hello?" Sally answered as the elevator doors opened onto the lobby.

"Where are you?" Marilyn asked sharply. "I've been trying to call you for the past two hours."

There was a note to the older woman's voice that Sally had never heard her use before. She identified it immediately as fear and felt her stomach drop.

"What's wrong?" she asked, getting straight to the point.

"It's your father. He came back into his office tonight, and security found him while they were on their rounds. He's had a heart attack and he's at the hospital now. It's bad, Sally, really bad."

A whimper escaped her as she took a mental note of the details of which hospital he was at.

"Where are you?" Marilyn asked. "I'll send Benton with the car."

"No, it's okay. I'm not far from the hospital. I've got a cab coming already. Are you there now?"

"Of course," the PA answered. A note of vulnerability crept into her voice. "But they won't tell me anything because I'm not next of kin."

"I'll be there as soon as I can. I promise."

Waiting for the cab was the longest five minutes of her life, and as it pulled away from the curb, Sally wondered how life could turn on the dime like that. How, in one moment, everything could be perfect and exciting and new, and in the next all could be torn away.

She should never have left her father after dinner tonight, especially on the eve of something as big as tomorrow's merger announcement. But how was she to know he'd go back into the office and, of all things, have a heart attack? And why had the security guards called Marilyn instead of her? Surely she, as his daughter, should have been listed on the company register as his immediate next of kin? But then, he'd always sheltered and protected her, hadn't he?

She remembered how drawn he'd looked tonight. How she'd dismissed it so easily as nothing out of the ordinary. She hadn't even asked if he was feeling ill. Guilt assailed her. He hadn't wanted to worry her about the merger, so why would he worry her about not feeling well? Suddenly her decision to be bold and chase after her own pleasure without thinking of the consequences tonight seemed horribly pathetic and selfish. If she'd simply gone home after her friends had left the bar, she'd have gotten the call and been at the hospital hours ago. What if she arrived too late? She didn't know what she'd do if she lost her dad. He was her rock, her mainstay, her shelter.

"Hold on, Daddy," she whispered. "Please, hold on."

Always an early riser, Kirk woke as sunlight began to filter through the blinds, his body satiated like it had never been before. He took a moment to appreciate the feeling and decided he could definitely go for another round of that. He reached across his sheets for Sally's warm, recumbent form beside him and came up with empty space. When had she pulled away from him? It wasn't like him to sleep so deeply that he couldn't remember his bed partner leaving, but then again he'd all but lost consciousness after the force of passion they'd shared.

Maybe she was in the bathroom. He looked across the bed to where light should have gleamed around the bathroom door frame, but there was only darkness. He sat up and cast his gaze around the room looking for her clothes. They were gone, as was she.

It shouldn't have mattered—after all, he knew he'd see her again at the office, even if she wasn't aware of that little detail just yet. But there was something almost shameful in the way she'd slipped out of his room without saying goodbye. As if she was embarrassed by what they'd done or wanted to pretend it hadn't happened.

Well, maybe it hadn't been as good for her as it was for him. He shook his head and told himself not to be so ridiculous. He knew she'd been there with him, every step of the way. Sometimes leading, sometimes allowing herself to be led. In fact, just thinking about her reactions—the sweet sounds she'd made, the responsiveness of her body beneath his touch—brought his desire immediately to full, aching life again.

Kirk groaned and pushed back the covers, remembering he hadn't rid himself of the condom he'd miraculously had the presence of mind to slip on last night. The groan rapidly turned into a string of wild curses when he realized the condom wasn't intact. He went to the bathroom and took care of what was left of it.

Now wide awake, several scenarios ran through his head. Of course, she could be on the Pill. Goodness only knew he hadn't stopped to ask. He'd barely stopped to put on protection himself, for all the good it had done. Either way, he had to tell her, and soon. He wondered how that would go. It's not like he could wait for her dad to introduce them at the office and shake her hand and say, "Hi, about last night… the condom broke."

He heard his cell phone ringing from the sitting room and walked, naked, to retrieve it from his suit jacket. He recognized the number as Orson Harrison's private line and answered immediately, surprised to hear a woman's voice, though she quickly introduced herself as Marilyn, Orson's assistant, and explained the medical emergency from the night before. His blood ran cold as he heard the news.

"Assemble the board as quickly as you can," he instructed Harrison's PA. "I'll be there in twenty minutes."

Three

Kirk's head was still reeling. At the emergency board meeting, everyone had been shocked to hear the news of Orson's heart attack, but all had agreed that the company could show no weakness, especially when Orson's confidential report on his reasoning behind the merger had been presented to them. Therefore, they'd appointed Kirk interim chairman.

The new responsibility was a heavy weight on him, along with worry for Orson Harrison's health. And on top of all that, he still had to tell Sally about the possibility she might be pregnant. He closed his eyes for a brief moment. He'd been such a fool to allow desire to cloud his judgment. It was the kind of impulsive emotion and need-driven behavior he'd always sworn he'd never indulge in. And now look where it had landed him.

He was investigating her, just as he was investigating every staff member here—he never should have allowed sex to muddy the waters.

He had no doubt she wouldn't be happy to hear his news. Who would be, especially while her father's life hung in the balance? So far the hospital had released very little information—only that Orson was in critical condition. Even Marilyn, who'd known Orson for almost thirty years, had been trying on the phone all morning, and remained unable to get past the gatekeeper of patient details at the hospital. To be honest, Kirk had been surprised to see the woman at her desk this morning and he'd expressed as much. She'd curtly informed him that someone had to hold the place together in Orson's absence and had been ill-pleased when she'd been informed of his appointment as interim chairman.

Kirk flicked a glance at his watch. Perhaps she'd gotten ahold of Sally again by now. He hit the inter-office button to connect with the prickly PA.

"Any updates regarding Mr. Harrison?" he asked.

"No, sir." The woman's voice was clipped.

She'd made it quite clear that she wasn't happy about him using Orson's office—interim appointment or not. She was even less impressed when he'd ignored her protests and taken up residence. It made sense to him to stand at the helm right now, when he was supposed to be steering this particular ship. It would help the staff to see someone visibly taking charge. Well, the staff except for Marilyn.

"Thank you, Marilyn," Kirk replied, keeping his voice civil. "And Ms. Harrison? Has there been any communication with her yet?"

"I believe she's in the building but I haven't spoken to her myself, yet."

Kirk looked at his watch. Two thirty. They were going forward with the planned announcement of the merger—it was, after all, the only thing that would explain why Kirk had taken temporary leadership—and the video link announcement was scheduled to commence at three sharp. Did Sally still plan to be there? He knew her father had wanted her by his side, but in light of recent events, he wouldn't blame her for skipping out. Coming into the office at all couldn't have been an easy decision to make with her father so desperately ill.

"Could you get a message to her and ask her to come to my office as soon as possible? I want to brief her before the video link."

"Certainly, sir."

Again there was that brief hesitation and slight distaste to her tone as she said the word *sir*. He'd already asked her to call him by his first name, but it seemed his request had been ignored. That, however, wasn't important to him right now. He had a far greater concern on his hands. Like, how the hell did he tell Sally about the condom?

It was only a few minutes before he heard women's voices outside the office door. The double doors began to swing open, and he heard Marilyn's voice call out in caution.

"Oh, but there's someone—"

And there she was. Sally Harrison appeared in the doorway, her head still turned to Marilyn, a reassuring smile on her face. A smile that froze then faded into an expression of shock when she saw him rise from behind her father's desk.

"K-Kirk?" she stammered.

Her face paled, highlighting the dark shadows of exhaustion and worry beneath her eyes that even makeup couldn't disguise. Kirk moved swiftly to her side, aware of Orson's PA coming up behind Sally. He gently guided Sally into a chair.

"A glass of water for Ms. Harrison, please, Marilyn," Kirk instructed the PA, who raced to do his bidding.

She was back in a moment, and Kirk took the glass from her before pressing it into Sally's shaking hand.

"Mr. Tanner, it's really too much to expect her to attend the video link," Marilyn began defensively. "She shouldn't have to—"

"It's entirely up to Ms. Harrison. Marilyn, perhaps you could get something for her to eat. I bet you haven't had anything today, have you?" he asked, looking at Sally directly.

Sally shook her head. "No. I couldn't bear to think about food."

She tried to take a sip of the water. Her hand was shaking so much Kirk wrapped his fingers around hers to steady her and keep her from spilling. She flinched at his touch, a reaction he was sure Marilyn hadn't missed.

"You need to eat something," he said. He turned to the PA. "Could you get a bowl of fruit from the executive kitchen for Ms. Harrison and perhaps some yogurt, as well?"

"Is that what *you* want, Sally?" Marilyn asked, moving to Sally's other side. "Perhaps you'd rather I stayed here with you while Mr. Tanner got you something to eat."

Kirk bit back a retort. He wasn't about to enter into a battle of wills with Marilyn here and now. And given the time constraints that now faced them, he wouldn't be able to have the discussion with Sally that they really needed to have. He studied her from the top of her golden head to her sensibly clad feet. Even in a demure pale blue suit and with her hair scraped back into a ponytail that gave him a headache just looking at how tightly it was bound, she still affected him.

Could she already be pregnant with his child? The thought came like a sucker punch straight to his gut.

"Good idea," he said, making a decision to leave their discussion until they could be guaranteed more privacy and uninterrupted time.

Of greater importance was letting Sally come to terms with his presence here—and the fact that he'd kept it from her last night. Once the shock wore off, he had no doubt matters between them would be less than cordial, especially once she discovered that he'd known exactly who she was all along.

Sally looked from him to Marilyn. "It-it's okay, Marilyn. You know what I like. Perhaps you could get it for me? I really am feeling quite weak."

"Of course you are," Marilyn said in a more placatory tone and patted Sally on the shoulder. "You've always had a delicate constitution. I'll be back in a moment."

Marilyn closed the door behind her with a sharp click, leaving Kirk in no doubt that even though Orson's PA had left the room to do his bidding, she certainly wasn't happy about it.

"Have another sip of water," he urged Sally.

He was relieved to see a little color coming back into her face.

"How is your dad doing?" he asked, determined to distract her until Marilyn's return.

She drew in another deep breath. "He's in an induced coma and they say he's stable—whatever that means. It's hard to see it as anything positive when he looks so awful and is totally nonresponsive." Her voice shook, but she kept going. "They're hoping to operate tomorrow. A quadruple bypass, apparently."

Kirk pressed a hand on her shoulder. "I know your dad. He's strong, he'll come through."

She looked up at him and he saw a flash of anger in her blue eyes.

"Just how well do you know my dad?"

Kirk felt a swell of discomfort, with just a tinge of rueful amusement. Trust Orson's daughter to cut straight to the chase. "I've known him most of my life, to be honest."

"And how is it I've never met you before last night?"

There was still a slight tremor to her voice, but he could see her getting stronger by the minute.

"Our parents were friends until my father died. After that my mom and I moved away. I was a kid at the time. There was no reason for you to know me before last night."

He kept it deliberately brief. There wasn't time for detail now.

"And now you're back." She fell silent a moment before flicking him another heated look. "You knew all along who I was, didn't you?"

Kirk clenched his jaw and nodded. He'd never been the kind of person who lived on regret, but right now, if he could have turned back the clock and done last night over again, he absolutely would have. Or would he? He doubted she'd have come home with him if she'd known he'd soon be her boss. Would he have missed the chance to lose himself in her arms the way he had? Never have known the perfect passion they'd experienced together? *Never had the broken condom*, the snarky voice in the back of his mind sharply reminded him. Okay, so he'd have skipped that part.

"I see." Sally swallowed another sip of water before speaking again. "She called you Mr. Tanner. That would be the Tanner in Harrison Tanner Tech? The new vice president?"

He nodded.

She pressed her lips together before speaking. "It seems you had me at a disadvantage right from the start. Which asks the question why you'd do something like that. Did it give you a kick to sleep with the chairman's oblivious daughter? Never mind—don't bother answering that."

Sally waved her hand as if to negate the words she'd just uttered.

"Look, can we talk about that later, over dinner?"

"I do not want to go out to dinner with you. In fact, I don't even want to be in the same room as you."

Her cheeks had flushed pink with fury. At least that was better than the waxen image she'd presented to him only a few moments ago.

Marilyn returned to the office and set a small tray on Sally's lap.

"There you are, my dear. Goodness knows, with your father so ill, the last thing we need is you collapsing, too. I've been telling your father for years now that he needs to slow down, but do you think he listens to me?" As if suddenly aware of the leaden atmosphere between Kirk and Sally, Marilyn straightened and gave Kirk a pointed glare. "Is there anything else…sir?"

"No, thank you, Marilyn. That will be all for now," Kirk replied. He flicked a quick look at his watch. "Eat up," he instructed Sally. "We have fifteen minutes."

"I don't feel like eat—"

"Please, Sally, at least try. It'll boost your blood sugar for now and hopefully tide you through the next few hours," Kirk said. "Whether you like it or not, we have to work together, today in particular. The last thing I want—and, as Marilyn already pointed out, the very last thing Harrison Tanner Tech needs—is you collapsing live on camera, especially during the merger announcement and even more so when news of your father's heart attack becomes public knowledge."

They locked gazes for what felt like a full minute before Sally acceded to his request and began to spoon up mouthfuls of the fruit.

"I still don't want to go out for dinner with you," she muttered between bites.

"We need to talk about last night, and we don't have time now."

"I don't particularly wish to discuss last night. In fact, I'd rather forget it ever happened."

Her words were cutting. Her anger and distrust right now felt like a palpable presence in the room. Such a contrast to the sweet openness she had shown him last night. And the tension between them was only going to get worse when she heard what he had to tell her. There was a knock at the door, and one of the communications team popped his head in.

"Ten minutes, Mr. Tanner! We need you miked and sound checked now."

"And me, too," Sally interjected in a shaking voice.

"Are you sure, Ms. Harrison?"

It wasn't Kirk's imagination—she paled again. But in true Harrison spirit, she placed her bowl on the desk in front of her and rose to her feet. She straightened her jacket and smoothed her hands over her rounded hips. Yes, there was still a tremor there.

"Absolutely certain. Let's get this over with," she said tightly.

"You don't have to speak. In fact, you don't have to do anything at all. I can handle the announcement."

"Really? Do you think that's a good idea given that people will be expecting to see my father? A man they know and *trust*—" she paused for emphasis "—and instead they're getting you?"

There was enough scorn in her voice to curdle milk.

"They can trust me," he said simply. "And so can you."

"You'll excuse me if I find that hard to believe."

Sally wished she hadn't eaten a thing. Right now she felt sick to her stomach. How dare Kirk have hidden his identity from her like that? What kind of a jerk was he? Was this some form of one-upmanship, lording his conquest over her before he'd even started here—making sure she knew exactly who was the top dog? And what if he tried to hold their one-night stand over her?

Sally stiffened her spine and looked him straight in the eyes. "In my father's absence, I would prefer to make the announcement regarding the merger.

You can fill in the details afterward. It's what Dad would want."

The sick sensation in her stomach intensified at the thought of being the figurehead for making the company-wide statement. But she could do this. She had to do this, to save face if nothing else. Kirk looked at her for a few seconds then shrugged and reached across the desk to grab a sheaf of papers. He held them out to her.

"Here's the statement your father prepared yesterday. If you're sure you can handle it, I have no objection to you making the announcement and then I'll field any questions from the floor. After the Q and A from the video feed closes, we'll repeat the same again for the press announcement."

"Why will you be answering questions? Why not Silas Rogers, the CEO, or any of our other senior management?"

"Sally, your father and I have been working together in the lead-up to this for several months now. No one else can give the answers I can. I'm the one who can carry out the plans your father and I made—that's why I've been appointed interim chairman. The board gave their approval at the meeting that was called this morning."

This morning. While she'd been at the hospital, out of her mind with worry over her father's condition. Her mind latched onto one part of what he'd said and yanked her out of her brief reverie.

"Several months?" Sally couldn't stop the outburst. "But I didn't hear about it until yesterday!"

"It was your father's decision to keep everything under wraps for as long as possible. Obviously he'd hoped to do the announcement with me today, present a united front and all that, but since he can't, we'll do the next best thing. Are you okay with that?"

Okay with it? No, she wasn't okay with it—any of it. But her dad had thought of everything, hadn't he? And none of it, except for a rushed dinner together last night, had included her.

"Sally?"

"Let me read the statement."

Sally scanned the double-spaced pages, hearing her father's voice in the back of her mind with every word she read. It wasn't right. He should be here to do this. This company was his pride and joy, built on his hard work, and he respected each and every one of his employees so very highly. Somehow she had to remember that in what she was about to do. Somehow she had to put aside her phobia and be the kind of person her father should have been able to rely on.

With every thought, she could feel her anxiety levels wind up several notches. *Be bold*, she told herself. *You can do this.* She drew in another deep breath then stood up and met Kirk's gaze.

"Right, let's go."

"Are you sure? You'll be okay?"

Blue-green eyes bored into hers, and she felt as though he could see through her bravado and her best intentions and all the way to the quivering jelly inside. He knew. Somehow, probably through her father, he knew about her glossophobia—the debilitating terror she experienced when faced with public speaking. Shame trickled down her spine, but she refused to back down.

"I'll be fine," she said, forcing a calm into her voice that she was far from feeling. "It's a video link, isn't it? Just us and a camera, right?"

"Look, Sally, you don't have to—"

She shook her head. "No, trust me, I really do."

He might not understand it, but this had become vital to her now. A method of proof that she was worthy. A way to show her father, when he was well enough to hear about it, that she had what it took and could be relied upon to step up.

Kirk gave her a small nod of acceptance. "Fine. Remember I'll be right beside you."

She'd been afraid he'd say that. But as they walked out of her dad's office and down the carpeted corridor toward the main conference room, she felt an unexpected sense of comfort in his nearness. She tried to push the sensation away. She didn't want to rely on this man. A man she knew intimately and yet not at all. *Don't think about last night! Don't think about the taste of him, the feel of him, the pleasure he gave you.*

She needn't have worried. Last night was the last thing on her mind as they entered the conference room and she was immediately confronted by the single lens of a camera pointing straight toward her. And beyond it was a bank of television screens on the large wall of the conference room—each screen filled with faces of the staff assembled at each of their offices. All of them staring straight at her.

Four

Kirk felt the shift in Sally's bearing the second they entered the conference room. He cast her a glance. She looked like she was on the verge of turning tail and running back down the corridor. She'd already come to a complete halt beside him, her eyes riveted on the live screens on the other side of the room, and he could see tiny beads of perspiration forming at her hairline and on her upper lip. And, dammit, she was trembling from head to foot.

"Sally?" he asked gently.

She swallowed and flicked her eyes in his direction. "I can do this," she said with all the grimness of a French aristocrat on her way to the guillotine.

Sally walked woodenly toward the podium set up in front of the camera. The sheaf of papers he'd given her earlier was clutched in one fist, and she made an effort to smooth them out as she placed them on the platform in front of her.

He had to give it to her. She wasn't backing down, even though she was obviously terrified. He wished she'd just give in and hand the papers back over to him. Making her go through this was akin to punching a puppy, and the idea made him sick to the stomach. Probably about as sick as she was feeling right now.

The camera operator gestured to Kirk to take the other seat and Kirk hastened to Sally's side. As he settled beside her, he could feel tension coming off her in waves. She'd grown even paler than when they'd arrived.

"Sally?" he asked again.

"Five minutes until we go live!" someone said from across the room. "Someone get mikes on them, please."

Kirk reached across and curved his hand around one of hers. "Let me do this. I've had time to prepare. You haven't."

He held his breath, waiting for her reply, but they were distracted by two sound technicians fitting them each with a lapel mike and doing a quick sound check.

"One minute, people."

Kirk squeezed her hand. "Sally, it's your call. No one expects this of you. Least of all your father—and especially given the circumstances."

"Don't you see," she whispered without looking at him. "That's exactly why I need to do it."

"Ten, nine, eight…"

"You only have to be here, Sally. That's more than enough given what you've been through."

"Live in three…" The technician silently counted down the last two numbers with his fingers.

Kirk waited for Sally to speak, but silence filled the air. Sally was looking past the winking red eye of the camera to the screens across the room, to the people of Harrison IT. Then, infinitesimally, she moved and slid the papers over to him. Taking it as his cue, Kirk pasted a smile on his face and introduced himself before he launched into the welcome Orson had prepared for his staff, together with a brief explanation that a medical event had precluded Orson from participating in the announcement.

Sally stood rigidly beside him throughout the explanation of the merger and the question-and-answer session that followed. The moment he signed off and the red light on the camera extinguished, Sally ripped off her microphone and headed for the door. He eventually caught up with her down the hallway.

"Leave me alone!" she cried as he reached for her hand and tugged her around to face him.

Kirk was horrified to see tears streaking her face.

"Sally, it's all right. You did great."

"Great? You call sitting there like a barrel of dead fish *great*? I couldn't even introduce you, which, in all honesty, was the very least I should have done given you are a total stranger to most of those people."

Distraction was what she needed right now.

"Dead fish? For the record, you look nothing like a barrel of anything, let alone dead fish."

She shook her head in frustration, but he was glad to see the tears had mostly stopped.

"Don't be so literal."

"I can't help it." He shrugged. "When I look at you, the last thing I picture is cold fish of any kind."

He lowered his voice deliberately and delighted in the flush of color that filled her cheeks, chasing away the lines of strain that had been so evident only seconds before.

"You're impossible," she muttered.

"Tell me how impossible over dinner after the press conference."

"No."

"Sally, we need to talk. About last night. About now."

He could see she wanted to argue the point with him, but he spied one of their media liaison staff coming down the corridor toward them. He was expected at the press conference right away.

"Please. Just dinner. Nothing else," he pressed.

He willed her to acquiesce to his suggestion. Not only did he need to talk to her about the broken condom, but he found himself wanting to get to know her better away from the confines of the office. He didn't realize he was holding his breath until she gave a sharp nod.

"Not dinner. But, yes, we can talk. I'm heading back to the hospital for a few hours first. I'll meet you later in my office. You can say what you have to say there."

It wasn't quite the acceptance he'd aimed for, but for now it would do. He watched her walk away and head to the elevators.

"Mr. Tanner, they're waiting for you downstairs in conference room three."

He reluctantly dragged his attention back to the job at hand. Unfortunately for him, Sally would have to wait.

It was late, and most of the staff had already headed home. The media session had run well over time, and afterward he'd been called into an impromptu meeting with the CEO and several others. The board might have agreed to appoint him interim chairman, but the executives still wanted to make it clear that they were the ones in charge. But he'd handled it knowing he had Orson's full support at his back, and that of the board of directors, too.

Now, he had a far more important task at hand. Kirk loosened his tie and slid it out from beneath his collar as he approached Sally's office. He bunched the silk strip into his pocket and raised a hand to tap at her door. No response. He reached for the knob, turned it and let himself in.

The instant he saw her, motionless, with her head pillowed on her arms on the top of her desk, he felt a moment of sheer panic, but then reason overcame the reaction and he noted the steady breathing that made her shoulders rise and fall a little. She'd removed her jacket before sitting at her desk, and the sheer fabric of her blouse revealed a creamy lace camisole beneath it.

Desire hit him hard and deep, and his fingers curled into his palms, itching to relieve her of her blouse and to slide his hands over the enticement that was her lingerie. He doubted it was quite as silky soft as her skin, but wouldn't it be fun to find out?

No, he shouldn't go there again. Wouldn't. Whatever it was about Sally Harrison that drew him so strongly, he had to rein it back. Somehow. It would be a challenge when everything about her triggered his basest primal instincts, but—he reminded himself—didn't he thrive on challenges and defeating obstacles? He forced himself to ignore the sensations that sparked through his body and focused instead on the reality of the woman sleeping so soundly that she hadn't heard him knock or enter her office.

She had to be exhausted. She'd been through a hell of a lot in the past twenty-four hours. Any regular person would have struggled with the onslaught of emotions, let alone someone forced to be part of a video conference who suffered a phobia like hers. Orson had forewarned him that Sally experienced acute anxiety when it came to public speaking. He'd had no idea how severe it was or the toll it obviously took. Having seen her like that today went a long way toward explaining why she'd remained in a safe middle-management role at HIT rather than scaling the corporate ladder to be at her father's side.

He'd never before seen such despair on a person's face at the thought of talking in public and, he realized, he'd never before seen such bravery as she'd exhibited in pushing herself to try. Perhaps if she hadn't been so emotionally wrung out, she'd have been in a stronger position to attempt to conquer her demons today. But she hadn't and, from their conversation in the hall, he knew she saw that as a failure.

He made an involuntary sound of sympathy, and she shifted a little on the desk before starting awake and sitting upright in her chair.

"What time is it?" she demanded defensively, her voice thick with exhaustion. "How long have you been waiting?"

There was a faint crease on her cheek where she'd rested her face on the cuff of her sleeve. Oddly, it endeared her to him even more. This was a woman who needed a lot of protecting—he felt it to the soles of his feet. She was the antithesis of the kind of women he usually dated, and yet she'd somehow inveigled her way into a nook inside him that pulled on every impulse.

"Not long," he answered. "And it's late. I'm sorry, I got held up. How was your dad?"

"As well as can be expected. He's still stable and continues to be monitored, and they're confident he'll come through the surgery well tomorrow."

As well as can be expected. It was an awful phrase, he thought, remembering hearing the exact same words from the medical team who had looked after his mother after the first of the strokes that stole her from him.

Sally pushed up from her desk and stood to face Kirk. "But you didn't come here to talk about him, did you? What did you want to say to me?"

"I was hoping we could discuss it over dinner. I don't know about you, but I'm starving after today."

"I thought we were going to talk here," she hedged.

"Can't we kill two birds with one stone?"

"Look—" she sighed "—is this really necessary? There's no need to spend an hour making small talk over a meal before we get to the point. We're both adults, so surely we can continue to act as such. I'm quite happy to forget last night ever happened."

Kirk ignored the sting that came with her words. He couldn't forget last night even if he wanted to—especially not now. "And, as adults, we should be able to enjoy a meal together. Really, I could do with a decent bite to eat, and I'm sure you could, too."

She looked at him and for a moment he thought she'd refuse, but then she huffed out a breath of impatience.

"Fine. I'll let my security know I'm leaving with you."

Ah, that explained the muscle who'd accompanied her to the bar last night. "You have security with you whenever you're out?"

"One of the examples of Dad's overprotectiveness. When I was little and HIT was beginning to boom, there was a threat to kidnap me. Ever since he's insisted on me having a bodyguard. Trust me, it's not as glamorous as it sounds."

"It's hardly overprotective," Kirk commented as he helped Sally into her suit jacket. "Your father clearly takes your welfare seriously."

He felt a pang of regret as she buttoned up the front of her jacket, hiding the tempting glimpses of lace visible through her blouse.

"He likes to know I'm safe."

"I protect what's mine, too," Kirk replied firmly.

Sally raised her eyebrow. "Isn't that a little primitive?"

"Perhaps I should rephrase that. Like your father, I take my responsibilities *very* seriously."

"Well, considering you're standing in for my father at the moment, I guess I should find that heartening."

Kirk smiled. "I will always do my best by the company—for your dad's sake, if nothing else. You can be assured of that. He has my utmost respect."

"You say you've known him most of your life, and yet I had no idea he even knew you. No idea at all." For a second she looked upset, but then she pulled herself together. "Let me call Benton and then we can go."

He could see it really bothered her that her father hadn't shared anything about the merger until the ink was drying on the paperwork. But was that because she was disturbed her father had made those decisions without consulting her, or because she had something to hide? Kirk couldn't be absolutely sure either way.

She made the call, and in the next few minutes they were riding the elevator to the basement parking. Kirk led the way to his car—a late-model European SUV.

"You must be relieved for your dad. That he's stable, I mean."

"I'll be relieved when I know he's getting better again." She looked away, but he couldn't mistake the grief that crossed her face. "He was so gray when I left him this afternoon. So vulnerable. I've never seen him like that. Not even when Mom died. And he still has a major surgery to get through."

"Your father has more strength and determination than any man I've ever met, and he'll be receiving excellent care at the hospital. He'll come through this, Sally."

The words seemed to be what she needed to hear to pull herself together again. She looked up and gave him a weak smile. For a second he caught a glimpse of the woman he'd danced with last night, but then she was gone again. Kirk waited for Sally to settle in the passenger seat and buckle her seat belt before he closed her door and went around to the other side. She was still pale, but she appeared completely composed and in control. Not quite the woman he'd met last night, but not the woman caught in the grip of the anxiety attack from this afternoon, either.

He pulled out of the parking garage and headed down the road.

"Any preference for dinner?"

"Something fast and hot."

"Chinese okay, then?"

"Perfect."

A few blocks down, he pulled into the parking lot for a chain restaurant he knew always had good food.

"Looks like this is us."

He rushed around to her door and helped her from the car and they were seated immediately.

"A drink?" he asked Sally when the waiter came to bring their menus.

"Just water, thank you."

Probably a good idea for both of them, he thought, and gave his request for the same to the waiter. "Do you mind if I order for us?"

Sally shook her head, and he turned to the waiter and requested appetizers to be brought out to their table as soon as possible and ordered a couple of main entrées to share, as well.

Her lips pulled into a brief smile. "You really are hungry, aren't you?"

Sally slipped out of her jacket and put it on the seat beside her. He looked at her across the table, noting again the imprint of her lacy camisole beneath her blouse. "You could say that," he replied with a wry grin.

Oh, yes, he was hungry for a lot of things, but only one of his desires would be satisfied by this meal tonight. To distract himself, he also shrugged off his jacket and undid the cuffs on his shirt and began to fold them back. He looked up and saw Sally's gaze riveted on his hands. Even in the dim light of the restaurant, he saw the rose pink stain that crept over her cheeks and her throat. Was she remembering exactly what parts of her body his hands had touched last night? Did she have any idea of how much he wanted to touch her again?

As if she sensed his gaze, she shook her head slightly and stared off into the distance, watching the other diners. Then, with a visible squaring of her shoulders, she returned her attention to him.

"Okay, so what was so important that you couldn't tell me at work?"

Kirk shifted in his chair. "It's about last night—" He paused, searching for the right words.

Sally felt her cheeks flush again. Did they really need to hash this all out? She'd much rather they just moved on.

"We covered this already," she interrupted. "Yes, it's awkward that we're working under the same umbrella after spending last night together. It happened, but it won't happen again. I'm sure we can be grown-up about it all and put it very firmly in the past. It doesn't have to affect our working relationship, such as it will be, and I'd prefer we just forget about it entirely."

She ran out of breath. Kirk eyed her from across the table.

"Are you quite finished?"

"Finished?"

"Your commendable little speech."

"Oh, that. Yes, I'm done."

"Great. I'd like to agree with you. However, we have a problem."

Sally looked at him in confusion. Did he think he couldn't work with her? She knew he'd mentioned redundancies in his announcement today. Surely he didn't mean to dismiss her from her job? Could he even do that? Was that what this dinner was about? Cold fingers of fear squeezed her throat shut.

"A problem?" she repeated.

"The condom broke."

Five

Of all the things he could have said, that was the last she'd expected. Sally felt the tension inside her coil up a few more notches. *The condom broke?* It kind of put her fear of redundancy in the shade, didn't it? She became aware that Kirk was watching her intently, waiting for her reaction. She forced herself into some semblance of composure. He'd seen her at her absolute worst already today—she couldn't afford to appear that weak to him again.

"Is that all?" She smiled tightly. "For a second there, I thought you were about to give me notice that you were terminating my job."

"You thought I was going to terminate you? Hell, no. But seriously, Sally—the condom. You have to let me know if—"

"You really have nothing to worry about," she interrupted him. She didn't want to hear him verbalize the words that were on the tip of his tongue. Didn't want to believe that pregnancy was a possibility, even though children were something she'd always desperately wanted. But not until it was the right time and, more importantly, with the right man. Certainly not with a man who would hide his identity and sleep with her while knowing exactly who she was.

"I'm on the Pill," she continued. "We're fine. Absolutely, totally and utterly fine."

"If you're sure?"

"One hundred and ten percent. Actually, no—just one hundred percent. One hundred and ten doesn't exist, really, does it? Percent meaning per hundred, right? So how can you have one hundred and ten hundredths?"

Darn, she was rambling. Nerves, combined with a healthy dose of anger, often did that to her in one-on-one conversation with people she didn't know well. It was a shame her phobia about public speaking didn't extend to rendering her mute in a situation like this, too. Kirk gave her a gentle half smile that made her stomach do a dizzy little flip, and beneath the lace cups of her bra she felt her breasts grow heavy and her nipples harden. Her body's helpless reaction to him served to stoke the fire of anger that simmered deep inside. He'd used her, she reminded himself.

"Okay then," he said with a gentle nod. "We're good. But if anything did happen, you'd let me know, right?"

"Of course," she answered blithely.

To her relief, the appetizers arrived and she helped herself to a lettuce wrap. She wasn't in the mood for small talk, and thankfully, now that Kirk had obviously gotten the business of the broken condom off his chest, he was far more invested in alleviating his hunger than indulging in idle chatter.

It didn't take long, though, before he steered conversation to work matters. It took a while to warm up to the discussion, and he seemed far more interested in asking questions than answering them, but overall she was surprised to find that Kirk agreed with and supported most of the principles she was passionate about for the company—especially her pet project of steering the head office at HIT, or HTT as it was now, toward more sustainable energy technologies and policies.

She wasn't certain if it was his skillful questioning or the energy burst she'd received from eating her first proper meal in twenty-four hours, but she found herself becoming quite animated as she delved deeper into her vision for the company.

"We could be leaders in this area if we do it right," she said passionately. "And with the correct systems set in place, we could take that platform to our clients, as well."

"Do it," Kirk said concisely.

"Do it?"

"Yeah. Draw up the proposal for me. I can already see how it would benefit us, but I'm not the only person you have to sell the idea to, right?"

This idea had been her baby from the outset, and she'd had a bit of pushback from a few of the senior managers when she'd floated it before. But getting the green light from Kirk was exciting, even if he was a low-down, deceitful piece of—

"I'll get onto it as soon as I can," she said. "I have most of the data assembled already."

"I look forward to seeing it," Kirk said. "Now, I think we've covered everything and it's probably time we headed home. You have an early start tomorrow, right?"

And just like that she hit the ground again. Her dad's surgery. How on earth could she have forgotten?

"Sally, don't feel bad. It's okay to escape now and then. Orson will come through this. You have to believe it."

Tears pricked her eyes, and she dragged her napkin to her lips in an attempt to hide their sudden quivering. After everything the last day had delivered, his unexpected compassion was just about her undoing. She blinked fiercely and put the napkin back down again.

"Thank you," she said. "Now, if you'll excuse me, I need to get a cab."

"No, I'll see you home. It's the least I can do."

She accepted his offer because she was absolutely too worn-out now to protest. She gave him her address and he smiled.

"Isn't that just a few blocks from the office?"

"It is. I like the building and it's close to Downtown Park when I need a blast of fresh air."

When they arrived at her apartment building, he rode the elevator with her to her floor.

"I'll be okay from here," she said as the elevator doors swooshed open.

"Let me see you to your door. It's what your guy—Benton?" he asked and waited for her nod before continuing "—would do, isn't it?"

She shrugged and walked down the hallway, hyperconscious of his presence beside her. Her hand shook as she attempted to put the key in the lock, and she almost groaned out loud at the clichéd moment when she dropped her keys and Kirk bent to retrieve them for her.

"Here, let me," he said.

Kirk suffered no such issues with his coordination, and he handed the keys back to her the moment the door was open. She looked up at him, all too aware of his strong presence beside her. Even though weariness tugged at every muscle in her body, she still felt that latent buzz of consciousness triggered by his nearness—and with it the tension that coiled tighter inside her with every moment they stood together. Suddenly all she could think about was the scent of him, the heat of his body, the sounds he'd made as she'd explored the expanse of his skin with her fingertips, her lips, her tongue.

She made a small sound and tried to cover it with a cough.

"You okay?" Kirk asked.

"I'm fine, thank you. And thanks for dinner, too."

"No problem."

Silence stretched out between them, and it seemed inevitable when Kirk lifted a hand to gently caress her face. The moment his fingers touched her skin, she was suffused with fire. *No*, she told herself frantically. She wasn't going down that road again. Not with him. She pulled back, and Kirk's hand fell to his side.

"Good night," she said as firmly as she could and stepped through the doorway.

"Good night, Sally. Sweet dreams."

She closed the door and leaned back against it, trying to will her racing heart back under control. One more second and she'd have asked him to stay. She squeezed her eyes shut tight, but it was no use. The image of him remained burned on her retinas.

Sally opened her eyes and went to her bathroom, stripping off her suit and throwing it in a hamper ready to send to the dry cleaner. She took a short, hot shower, wrapped herself up in her robe and went to her bedroom. Perched on her bed, she opened her handbag, pulling out the blister pack of contraceptives she carried everywhere with her.

She studied the pack, then flipped it over to check the days. Her chest tightened with anxiety the moment she realized that somewhere along the line she'd gotten out of sync. Probably around the time a couple of weeks ago when she'd traveled to the small European kingdom of Sylvain for the christening of the baby of her best friend from college. With the time zone changes and the busyness of travel and jet lag and then getting back to work, she'd slipped up. Normally, it wouldn't have been a problem—it wasn't as if she was wildly sexually active. But it certainly was a problem now.

She couldn't be pregnant. She simply couldn't. The chances were so slim as to be nearly nonexistent, weren't they? But the evidence of her inconsistency stared straight at her from the palm of her hand.

Sweet dreams, he'd said. How could she dream sweet dreams when every moment had just become a waking nightmare?

It had been four weeks since her father's surgery, and despite a minor post-op infection in a graft site on his leg, everything had gone well. He was home now, with a team of nurses stationed around the clock to ensure his convalescence continued to go smoothly. Sally bore his daily grumbles with good humor—especially when, as each bland meal at home was served to him, he called her to complain about the lack of salt and other condiments he'd grown used to.

She was too relieved he was still alive and getting well again to begrudge him his complaints. He still had a way to go with his recovery, despite how well he was doing, but it was ironic that each day he seemed to have more energy, while each day she had less.

She chalked it up to the hours she was working. After all, what with juggling expanding the proposal for sustainable strategies she'd discussed with Kirk the night before her father's operation and daily visits to her father on top of her usual duties here at the office, it was no wonder she was feeling more tired than usual.

She was no longer worried about the broken condom or the mix-up with her Pill. She knew people who'd tried for years to get pregnant. The odds of her having conceived after just that one encounter with Kirk…? No, she wasn't even going to think about that again. For her own peace of mind, a couple of weeks ago she'd taken a home test and it had showed negative—to her overwhelming relief. She was just tired. That was all. Things would settle down after the presentation, she told herself.

It had become vital to her to make her presentation better than her best effort. She had no room for error on this. There were plenty of people in the office who were on the fence about the whole concept of energy technology and sustainability in the workplace. All it would take was a slipup from her and a damning comment from the chief executive officer, Silas Rogers—who she knew already disagreed with her on principle—and no matter how much support she had from Kirk, the concept would be dead in the water.

It had been interesting these past couple of weeks, watching people react to Kirk being installed as interim chairman in her father's absence. There was a fair amount of wariness interspersed with the obvious suck-ups who wanted to ensure that their jobs would remain secure in the merger transition that would take place over the next twelve months. And maybe that was another reason she wanted to make this presentation flawless. If it went ahead, she'd be project manager, and her own position and those of her team would be secure, too. And maybe, just maybe, she'd be able to prove to herself and to her father that she had what it took.

Another week later and Sally was finally satisfied she had everything in place. She'd booked the conference room on the executive floor, she'd gone through her PowerPoint, tested transmitting it to her team's portable devices and rehearsed her part of the presentation until she could recite everything forward, backward and in Swahili. Okay, so maybe not in Swahili, but she knew her stuff and so did her team.

For all that they were an information technology company, there were several diehards among the senior management who still preferred a paper handout to reading a handheld screen. After today she hoped to change that. She was so excited about seeing her team put forward the full development of their ideas. It could mean such wonderful things for Harrison Tanner Tech long-term that she hadn't even had time to feel anxious about talking in front of a group. Granted, it wouldn't be a huge crowd and she knew every person who would be there, but that hadn't stopped her phobia from taking over before. This time, though, felt different. She felt as though she could really do this, and her veins fizzed with anticipation as opposed to the dread she usually felt.

Sally had taken extra care with her appearance that morning, choosing a dress she knew flattered her. Her hair was pulled back into its customary ponytail, and her makeup was perfectly understated. Kirk would be at the presentation. She felt a flush of color steal into her cheeks. She had barely seen him since the night they'd had dinner together, although they had spoken on the telephone. He'd said it was to check for updates on her father's recovery, but she had a suspicion that it had more to do with his concerns about their failed contraception. Her notion was backed up when the calls stopped after she'd told him about the home test result.

She knew Kirk had been in and out of meetings and had spent some time back in California, finalizing things for his move to Seattle. It had filtered through the grapevine—not without a few remarks, both envious and full of admiration—that he'd bought a lakefront property here in Bellevue. She'd been relieved that their paths hadn't had to cross.

A chime at her door told her that Benton was there to take her to work. As soon as she arrived in the HTT building, she went straight to the main conference room on the senior management floor. It was time to slay her demons. The last time she'd been here—for the video feed announcing the merger—she'd made a complete idiot of herself in front of Kirk, not to mention all the staff. She'd heard one or two comments, hastily hushed, as she'd gone by in the office. While some people knew she held her position here in her father's firm purely on merit, there were a handful, including the CEO, who made their thoughts on nepotism perfectly clear.

She had so much to prove today. Normally, such a realization would have been daunting, but right now she felt completely in control. Sally looked around the room and silently approved the layout that she'd requested together with the screen that had been set up in readiness. She did a quick run-through with her tablet. Everything was working perfectly. She had this.

Over the next thirty minutes, the chairs slowly filled up as senior managers made their way into the room. There was a hum of activity when Kirk arrived, and Sally found herself holding her breath in anticipation as he walked toward her to say hello.

Her nostrils flared slightly as he neared, the delicious scent of him sending a tingle through her body. A tingle she instantly did her best to quash.

"Good morning," she said, pulling together all the smoothness she could muster. "I hope your trip back to California was successful."

"It was, thank you." His eyes raked over her and her heart rate picked up a notch or two. "And you've been okay?"

"Just fine," she replied with a smile fixed to her face.

"Tanner, good to see you back."

Kirk turned to acknowledge Silas Rogers, who she knew couldn't wait to see her fail. He'd never liked her, and she could see that despite the congenial look pasted on the man's face, he resented Kirk's presence here, too. After all, he would have been the natural fill-in for her father during his illness and recovery had it not been for the board's appointment of Kirk.

Sally cast a glance at one of her team and gave them her signal to commence. She'd decided to keep her speaking role strictly limited to explaining the concept she wanted to see the company adopt in their head office and how it could be expanded over the next five years through all their branches. As soon as her second in charge, Nick, was finished with his spiel, she was ready to whirl into action.

A tricky little wave of nausea surged through her. Sally reached for her water glass and took a sip then breathed in deeply. Nick was beginning to wind up his introduction, and all eyes would soon be turning to her. Her armpits prickled with perspiration, and another wave of nausea swelled. Again she took a small sip of water then focused on her breathing. The sick feeling subsided. She let a sense of relief flow through her. She could do this.

"…and without further ado, here's our team leader, Sally Harrison, to fill you in on why we're all so excited about what this proposal will do for HTT now and in the future. Sally?"

She rose to her feet, tablet in hand, and started her spiel. If she kept her eyes fixed between the projector screen and her tablet, she could even pretend there were no other people in the room.

The first few minutes of her presentation went extremely well, as she explained why it was important for HTT to evaluate the energy technologies available to them, and the next stage started brilliantly as she showed how going paperless in the office was one small step on the ladder. She demonstrated how they'd implemented the change in her department alone, and the figures she quoted showed the significant savings this had brought—not to mention the diminished waste footprint left on the environment.

"So you can imagine the long-term impact this will have on an entire floor, the entire head office and especially each and every HTT office around the globe."

There was a general murmur of assent from about seventy percent of the assembly. Sally took another breath and continued with her presentation.

"Small, consistent changes made on a wide scale is what we need. Can you imagine how something as simple as replacing the current management motor fleet with hybrid vehicles and installing solar panels on the rooftop of the HTT building to feed energy back into the grid would reduce the company's carbon footprint? And while there would be some initial costs, in the end all these steps would significantly reduce our overall expenses."

She was heading into the homestretch when a vicious wash of dizziness struck, and she faltered in her speech and put a hand out to steady herself. Kirk spoke from his position a couple of yards away from her.

"Sally? Everything okay?"

She pulled her lips into a smile and made her eyes flare open wide. Anything to stop the influx of black dots that now danced across her vision. She'd had her share of panicked reactions to public speaking, but this was new…and a little frightening. What was wrong with her? And would she be able to hide it until the presentation was complete?

"I'm fine," she said, but her voice was weak.

She looked at the people sitting there, all of them with eyes trained on her. Saw the smirk on Silas Rogers's face. And then she did the unthinkable. While she stared directly into Kirk's face, her tablet fell and bounced on the carpet, and she followed it down, sliding to the floor in an ignominious and unconscious heap.

Six

Kirk acted on instinct. He scooped Sally into his arms.

"Finish the presentation," he instructed the nearest member of her team as concerned murmurs swirled around them. "She's counting on you."

Then, without wasting another second, he stalked out of the room and down the corridor to Orson's office.

"What's wrong with Sally?" Marilyn asked, rising to her feet as he came into the executive suite.

"She collapsed."

"We have a nurse on duty for the staff here. I'll call her."

"Yes, do that, thanks."

He laid Sally down on a couch. Thankfully she was beginning to regain consciousness.

"Wha—?"

"You fainted," Kirk filled in as she looked around her. "At least I think you fainted. I want you to go to the hospital for tests to make sure it's not anything serious."

Sally tried to struggle to an upright position. "Go to the hospital? Don't be ridiculous. I'll be fine. I need to get back in there. I have to finish what I started."

He could understand why she felt that way. A little research had revealed that Sally's fear of public speaking had held her back from advancing within the company, purely because she'd been unable to speak to any size group in a situation like the one today. That she'd done as well as she had this morning had surprised him. Even more surprising was how proud of her he'd felt while she was doing it.

If he hadn't been so focused on getting her out of the conference room, he would have stopped to wipe that ridiculous expression off Rogers's face. He made a mental note to have a word with the man about the aside he'd heard him make about Sally riding on others' coattails, implying that she was incapable of completing anything on her own. There was so much more to her than that narrow-minded stuffed shirt realized…so many depths to Sally Harrison that Kirk, in spite of himself, wanted to explore.

Over the past five weeks, he'd tried to tell himself that the crazy attraction between them was just that. A moment of craziness and nothing more. But seeing her this morning had brought his attraction to her back to the fore again. He'd resented having to turn and say hello to that pompous idiot Rogers when he'd finally gotten the chance to see her face-to-face again. Add to that the sheer panic that flew through him as she lost consciousness and hit the carpeted floor of the conference room, swiftly followed by the instinctive need to protect her, and he knew that the way he felt about Sally Harrison was more than crazy. It was downright certifiable.

A movement at the door alerted him to the arrival of the staff nurse, with Marilyn close on her heels.

"I have some water for her," Marilyn said, putting a fresh pitcher and a glass on the side table.

"Nothing by mouth until we know what we're dealing with," said the nurse firmly but with a friendly smile. "Now, Ms. Harrison, how about you tell me what happened?"

The woman efficiently unpacked the small bag she'd brought with her and put a blood pressure cuff on Sally's arm while taking her temperature with a digital ear thermometer. Sally briefly outlined how she'd felt in the moments before she fainted. Kirk could see she was embarrassed, but he wasn't taking any risks by letting her brush this off. A suspicion began to form in his mind.

"Blood pressure is a little low. Temperature is normal. So you say you felt some nausea before you collapsed?"

Sally flicked her eyes to Kirk and then back to the nurse. "Yes, just a little. It's not unusual for me to feel that way, especially when talking to a large group. I'm okay with my team, but this was an important presentation and, I guess, I may have let that get to me."

"You've fainted before while speaking?" Kirk asked before the nurse could ask the same question.

"Not exactly. Usually I just feel sick and freeze. Today was different. But then again, today I actually got through a lot of my presentation. I was doing okay up until that dizzy spell hit."

"You were doing great," Kirk reassured her. "And your team is well trained and will do a fabulous job going through the rest of it in your absence. Don't worry about it."

"But—" she began in protest.

"Sally, I know you want to blame this on your difficulties with speaking in public, but given the situation with your father's health I'm going to insist you still go to the hospital to rule anything else out. HTT cannot sustain any weakness in any department right now."

His voice was sharper than he'd intended, and he forced a smile to his lips to soften his words. Thing was, his statement was truer than she probably realized. HTT was vulnerable right now, in more ways than one. He'd received news today that another major contract had been lost to their main rival. It made him all the more determined to find the wretched mole who continued to undermine HTT's every potential new success.

Sally looked at him, and he watched as the light of defiance left her soft blue eyes. "Fine," she said through gritted teeth. "But I don't want to go to hospital. It'll take far too long. I agree to going to either an urgent care clinic or my own doctor and I'm coming back to work straight afterward."

"That will depend entirely on the outcome of your examination," he replied firmly.

She rolled her eyes at him, but he wasn't about to be swayed. If what he suspected was confirmed…? No, she'd said she'd taken a test. Said the results were negative. But home testing wasn't always a hundred percent accurate, was it?

He couldn't jump the gun. They'd wait until she'd seen a doctor, had some tests, then they'd deal with what came next.

The nurse agreed with Sally that a hospital visit wasn't necessary and, after a quick discussion, agreed Kirk should transport her to the nearest clinic. After their arrival there, nothing could dislodge Kirk from her side, and in the end it had been easier to simply allow him to be there in the treatment room with her, especially since she suspected he wouldn't trust her to deliver the results in full when she got them. That said, when the doctor returned after what felt like an interminable wait, to deliver the results of the first run of tests, she felt strangely relieved to have Kirk by her side.

"Okay, Ms. Harrison, you're a little anemic, but that's not unusual in your case. Overall you're in excellent health, and I'm going to discharge you. It's going to be important that you not skip meals and that you take some supplements to counter the anemia, and I want you to make sure that you get plenty of rest and fluids."

"Hold on," Sally said, putting up a hand. "Not unusual in my case? Why? I've never been anemic before. Yes, I've been busy lately and under a bit of stress, but why would that lead to anemia?"

"Did the nurse not let you know?"

"She hasn't been back. Let me know what?" Sally's voice rose in frustration, but Kirk had a feeling he knew exactly what the doctor was going to say.

"You're pregnant," the doctor said without preamble.
Bingo.

Kirk listened while Sally argued with the doctor, insisting that it couldn't be true, but apparently the proof was right there in the test results. Kirk said nothing, just let the news sink in. He'd been relieved when Sally had told him the home test had been negative. Hugely relieved. His life plan had been in the making from when he was in his early teens, and he'd seen no reason to ever veer from that. Marriage and children were far down the line in his ten-year plan. And yet…

He was going to be a daddy. The words resonated through his mind over and over. Together with the woman on the hospital bed, a woman he'd been completely unable to resist the night they'd met, he was going to be a parent. Sally, it seemed, was having an even harder time than him in accepting the news.

"I can't be pregnant," Sally said again, this time more adamantly than before. "It was only that one time."

"That's all it takes sometimes, I'm afraid. Perhaps I could refer you for some counseling?" the doctor said.

"I don't need counseling. I just don't see how this could have happened."

"Look, we'll deal with it together," Kirk hastened to reassure her.

"I guess we'll have to," she replied bitterly. "I didn't want this."

"I didn't plan for it, either," he agreed. "But now that we're faced with it, we can make plans."

And they *would* make plans. There was no way he was missing out on his child's life the way his father had missed out on his. His father's descent into drug addiction had seen him not only lose his position as the development manager for Harrison IT in its earliest incarnation, it had also resulted in Frank Tanner's death by suicide several years later—leaving his twelve-year-old son and his wife with more questions than answers and very little money to make ends meet. If it hadn't been for Orson Harrison's assistance, who knew where they'd have ended up?

No, his child would not go without—neither emotionally nor materially.

"Can I go back to work now?" Sally asked the doctor, interrupting Kirk's train of thought.

"Of course. Pregnancy isn't an illness, but I'd like you to reduce stress and get into a good routine ensuring you eat properly and regularly, take prenatal vitamins, and fit a little exercise into each day if you don't already."

"Surely you don't want to go back to work today," Kirk stepped in before Sally could respond. "Your body has had a shock. Take the day to recover fully."

She gave him a scathing look. "You heard the doctor. I'm pregnant, not sick. Besides, I need to get back to my team and find out the result of the Q and A after the presentation."

Kirk knew when to pick his battles, and this definitely wasn't one he'd be able to win. Better to give in gracefully rather than cause a scene in front of the medical center staff.

"Fine, we'll head back."

"Thank you."

Although she'd said the words with every nuance of good manners, he could sense the sarcasm beneath them. She was used to making her own decisions, and she wasn't going to accept him telling her what to do. He was going to have to become inventive if he was going to achieve his objectives with respect to being there for her and their baby. That was fine. He was nothing if not inventive.

They took a cab back to the office, barely speaking. Clearly Sally was still digesting the news about the baby, but this would be the last time she'd be doing any of it on her own—he'd make certain of that. Still, it wasn't the kind of discussion he wanted to have in the back of a cab, so he'd have to shelve it until they could be alone together again.

While he took care of paying the cab driver, Sally made her way into the building, and he managed to catch up with her by the elevators.

"In such a hurry to get back to work?"

"This is important to me, Kirk. It might have escaped your notice, but I'm the boss's daughter. As such, people either treat me as if I'm their best friend because they think being nice to me will advance their career, or I'm their archenemy because they think I'll run back to Dad and narc on them for any minor transgression—or you, now, since Dad's still recuperating. Many think I shouldn't be here at all. I have to work twice as hard and twice as long as anyone here for people to take me seriously, and all my hard work is probably ruined now thanks to fainting during the presentation today."

"I'm sure you're exaggerating."

"You think? Aside from my team and Marilyn, there are very few people here who believe I'm capable of doing the job I was hired to do. Yes, *hired*. I applied for that position just like anyone else, and that was after interning here during my summer and semester breaks as often as my father would let me."

"If it's all so hard, why bother? Why not go elsewhere? You are eminently employable. You have a sharp mind and great ideas. Any company would be lucky to have you," Kirk hastened to assure her.

He already knew a lot of what she'd just told him about her credentials and experience, but he'd had no idea that she was a pariah to so many, as well.

"Because my father started this business. It's in my blood, and as such I feel invested in it, too. And while I'll probably never be good enough to take over the company when he's ready to retire, like I always dreamed of when I was younger, the company and my father deserve my best—not some other nameless, faceless corporation."

The elevator doors opened onto Sally's floor, and she stepped out.

"Sally, wait. We need to talk about this."

"Thank you for your help today," she said, holding the elevator door open. "Call me and make an appointment if you want to talk. Right now it's—"

Her voice broke off, as if she couldn't even bring herself to discuss the child now growing in her belly.

"It's just too complicated," she continued, her cheeks flushing.

With that, she let the door close, and he caught a last glimpse of her walking away. Kirk wanted to refute her statement. It wasn't complicated as far as he was concerned. She was pregnant with his baby, and that meant they had a future together whether she realized it or not.

With the chemistry they shared, being together would be no hardship. But it seemed he had to convince her of that. He'd let her think she'd had the last word on the subject, that she had the upper hand. And then he'd try to change her mind.

Sally fielded the multitude of queries about her health in a convincing facade of good humor as her team gathered around her.

"I'm fine. I'd just been burning the candle at both ends and skipping a few too many meals. You know how important this project was to all of us. Everything else went on the back burner for me when it came to this. So, Nick, how did it go?"

"The presentation went really well. I'd say the majority of the managers there seemed very interested in exploring the concept further and starting to implement the changes. Everyone could see that it was a time- and money-saver in the long-term, even though initial outlay in replacing what we're already using, especially the motor fleet, will be costly."

There was something in Nick's tone that made Sally's stomach clench.

"And did they vote on implementation?"

Nick fell silent, and one of the other members of Sally's team filled the silence.

"Before they could vote, Mr. Rogers spoke up."

"I see." A ripple of frustration cascaded through her mind, but she couldn't let her people know how the news upset her. "I take it he's not a fan of the suggested changes, then?"

Her staff looked at her with the same disappointed expression she was certain was on her own face and, as a group, shook their heads. Some things just didn't bear saying out loud.

"So we need to work harder, then. Tackle this from another perspective."

"That won't be necessary."

Sally wheeled around to find Kirk standing behind her, fistfuls of takeout bags clutched in his hands. Couldn't he leave her alone for a second?

"And why not?" she challenged, ready to do battle.

"Because there's nothing wrong with the perspective you presented. Here," he said, putting the takeout bags on the meeting table in front of them. "I heard you guys haven't had a break for lunch yet, so it's on me. From what I saw you've put a great deal of planning into this project, and I'd like to see it developed further."

"And Silas Rogers?"

"Is not the chairman of HTT, nor is he interim chairman of HTT."

"He's still the CEO, and what he says carries weight," Sally argued.

"That's true," Kirk admitted and pulled up a chair to sit beside her. He ripped open a takeout bag and passed her a sub filled with salad fixings and well-done hot roast beef. "Eat, then we'll discuss this some more."

Sally bristled at his high-handedness, but her mouth began to water at the smell of the sub, and hunger won the war over pride. She reluctantly took it from him and sank her teeth into the fresh bread, groaning in appreciation as the flavors of the fillings burst on her tongue. She hadn't realized she was quite so hungry.

Next to her, she felt Kirk stiffen and shift in his chair. He tugged at the front of his trousers and pulled a napkin across his lap, but not before she saw evidence of a hint of arousal pressing against the fine Italian wool of his suit. Shock rippled through her, accompanied by a powerful wave of something else—desire. No, no, no. She wasn't going to go there again. No way. Never.

Even though she scolded herself soundly, she couldn't help the prickle of heat that crept through her, couldn't prevent the surge of sheer lust that forced her inner muscles to clench involuntarily. It was a turn-on to know that she was capable of arousing an attractive man without even trying. And while she had a whole list of problems with this particular man, there was no denying he was gorgeous—he had a body like a Greek god and he knew exactly how to use it. All of it. His mouth, his tongue, those hands and especially—

No! She squirmed in her seat.

"Is your lunch okay?" Kirk asked with a curious expression on his face.

"Great," she said, taking another bite, this time with less audible enthusiasm.

She'd have to eat more carefully in the future, she decided, if enjoying her sub had this effect on him. And if his reaction had the same domino effect on her. So she'd have to remember to control herself. That couldn't be too hard, could it? She had no plans to eat with him again after this, did she? In fact, she had no plans to spend any more time with him than their jobs absolutely required.

For some stupid reason, that thought caused a pang of something deep inside—something she didn't quite want to define. *He lied to you*, she reminded herself. By omission, yes, but keeping his true identity from her that night had been deliberate, and she still had no idea why he'd done it or what he'd hoped to gain by it. *So ask him*, the little voice at the back of her mind said pragmatically.

Maybe she would. But that would mean spending

more time together, wouldn't it? Besides, referring to that night would bring back the memories of how she'd behaved so uncharacteristically. Of what they'd done—and of how it had made her feel.

Darn it! Maybe it was hormones, she thought. She'd never been the type to play sex kitten. In fact, she'd always been slightly embarrassed and a little uncomfortable when the girls around her in college, and even sometimes here in the office, ever discussed their sexual activities. But there was something about this guy that opened sensual floodgates she hadn't known existed. She'd always thought that maybe she was just slightly different from the other women she knew—less passionate, less sensual. But maybe she'd just been waiting for the right man to come along.

Except he wasn't the right man, was he? He was her boss. He was a sneak. And yet he was the best lover she was ever likely to have in her lifetime.

She sighed and put down her now empty wrapper. She'd been so caught up in her thoughts that she hadn't even realized she'd finished the sub.

For the next several hours, Kirk chaired a discussion between Sally and her team on the best way to begin implementing the proposal. By the end of the workday, she didn't know if she was energized because she was so excited about seeing her spark of an idea being set on the road to fruition or exhausted at the thought of all the work ahead. She did feel a deep sense of satisfaction, though, and she'd begun to see Kirk in a new light.

He had that rare talent of listening—and listening well—to what her team had to say. And when he injected his own thoughts and ideas, he was gracious about accepting criticism if those ideas were challenged. A part of her wished she'd never met him that night, that instead she'd had the chance of meeting him in the normal course of work and of seeing whether the attraction that crackled between them like static electricity might have grown naturally over time rather than exploding all at once in the accelerated fling they'd had.

But now they were linked by a baby. Her mouth turned dry as sawdust. While she wanted to have as little to do with Kirk as possible, she would never deny her child access to their father. The very thought was impossible to her, especially when her own relationship with her dad was such an integral part of who she was. But how could they coparent a child when there was still so much tension between them?

Maybe she was getting ahead of herself. She had plenty of time to think about all that. Plenty of time to work out adequate coping strategies and discuss this situation they had found themselves in like rational adults. People did that all the time, didn't they?

But did they spend half their time fighting a magnetic pull so strong she felt like a helpless tide being influenced by a supermoon? She didn't want to think about that right now. She'd have to put it on the back burner for as long as she could. But, judging by the quick glances flung her way by the man sitting next to her, that wouldn't be very long at all.

Seven

The meeting finished and Kirk hung back, talking to Nick, as Sally gathered her things together and stopped to give instructions to a handful of people. He liked watching her in action. Hell, he liked watching her, period. As if she sensed his perusal, she looked up and caught his eye. And, yes, there was that telltale flush of color on her cheeks. He was finding it more and more endearing each time he saw it.

Finally she was ready to leave, and he fell into step with her as she headed to the elevators.

"Feeling okay?"

She rolled her eyes. "I'm fine, seriously. There's nothing wrong with me."

"You're carrying my baby," he murmured close to her ear. "I think I'm entitled to be concerned."

She stiffened at his words. "So, what? You want to monitor me twenty-four-seven? Is that what it is?"

The idea had merit.

Sally huffed an impatient sigh. "Look, it's still early, and I can assure you I will do whatever is in my power to stay healthy and to ensure that everything goes as it should."

Somehow that didn't satisfy him. For reasons even he didn't understand, it just didn't go far enough.

"I'm sure you will," he agreed. "But you have to admit, sharing that responsibility has its advantages, too."

"What do you mean?" she asked as they stepped into the empty elevator.

"I don't know if you've been sick yet, but what if nausea does occur?"

"Then I'll deal with it," she said grimly and crossed her arms over her body. "I'm a big girl, Kirk. I've been looking after myself for a good many years now. I think I can cope with a pregnancy."

"I've no doubt. But I'd really like to be a part of things. I know this news has come as a shock to both of us, but I'd like to think that together we can get through it. Look, can I see you home so we can talk about this in a more private setting?"

Sally rolled her eyes at him. "You're not going to leave me alone until I agree, are you?"

He didn't want to leave her alone at all. The thought came as a shock, but it felt right at the same time.

"I like to get my way," he conceded. "But I'd feel

happier if you conceded that this is something we should iron out sooner rather than later."

"Oh, of course, your being happy is so very important," she said with a touch of bitterness. "Okay, then. You can take me home. Benton will be waiting downstairs for me. I'll have to let him know."

It was a small victory, but Kirk was happy to take it. Benton was waiting in the elevator lobby of the parking garage, and Kirk stepped forward to introduce himself. The man looked him over as if he was a potential threat before relaxing an increment when Sally stepped forward with an apologetic smile.

"I'm sorry I couldn't give you notice of this, Benton. Mr. Tanner and I need to extend our discussions, so he'll be taking me home this evening."

"Whatever you want, Ms. Harrison. I'll see you in the morning, then?"

"Yes, thank you."

Kirk walked Sally over to his SUV and helped her in.

When they arrived at her apartment building a few minutes later, he pulled into the parking space she indicated. They rode the elevator to the top floor, and he followed her into an elegant and well-proportioned apartment. While it was mostly decorated in neutral tones, an occasional pop of color drew his eye—a cushion here, a throw rug there. But overall there was very little to tell him about the woman who intrigued him far more than he wanted to admit.

He moved to the large windows that looked out in the direction of Lake Washington. It was growing dark, and across the lake he could make out the twinkle of lights around its rim. A sound from behind him made him turn. Sally had pulled the band from her hair and was tousling her fingers through the mass of spun gold. He liked this more relaxed version of her more than the buttoned-down woman who headed her social engineering department. On second thought, he liked the naked, warm and willing version from just over a month ago the best, but she'd made it quite clear they weren't going to go there again.

But it was oh so satisfying, he reminded himself. *And yet look at the trouble it has put us in*, he countered. Kirk slammed the door closed on his thoughts and looked at Sally more closely. Beneath her makeup he could still see the telltale signs of the stress she'd been under today. She had to be exhausted.

"Look, I won't take up a lot of your time. I know you need to get something to eat and then probably have an early night."

She barked a cynical laugh. "Are you my mother now?"

He gave her a half smile of apology. "I'm sorry, I guess I'm overcompensating."

"You think?" She moved toward the kitchen. "Did you want something to drink? I have beer, water, wine."

"A beer, thanks."

He watched as she poured the beer into a tall glass then opened a small bottle of sparkling water for herself. Of course she wouldn't be drinking alcohol. The realization hit him hard. She was going to have to make so many changes. So many adjustments. It was hardly fair, was it?

"Take a seat," she said, bringing their drinks through to the small sitting room.

Kirk sat at one end of the sofa, and Sally took the other end. Awkward silence stretched between them.

"You wanted to talk, didn't you? What about, exactly?" Sally asked.

"The baby, for a start. How do you feel about it?"

"Shocked, surprised. Scared."

"Yeah, me too. I hadn't planned on this at this stage of my life."

Sally sat a little more upright. "And just when had you planned it for?"

He couldn't tell if she was sniping at him or genuinely curious. He decided that honesty was probably the best policy right now.

"To be honest, I had hoped to start looking for a wife about five years from now and hopefully start a family a few years after that."

"Just like that?"

"Look, I know it sounds clinical, but I grew up with a lot of instability. Being able to make a plan and stick to it kept me anchored when things were tough at home, even when my dad was still alive." He didn't want to admit his father's weakness to her. He'd spent his entire adult life working hard to erase those memories, to overcome the hardships he and his mother had endured—and he'd succeeded.

He wasn't about to be made to feel ashamed of that. Not by anyone.

Sally shrugged and took a sip of her water. "That makes sense, I guess. I'm sorry things were so hard for you."

"You know that saying about gaining strength through adversity? Well, I decided to adopt that a long time ago. And I've managed to achieve a lot of success by staying strong and keeping my focus on my goals. But now I need to reevaluate. This child we're having, I very much want to be a part of its life, Sally. I don't want to be a weekend father or an absentee parent. I want to be there, for everything."

"That could be difficult, considering we're not even a couple."

"But we could be. We already know we're compatible in the bedroom."

"Too compatible, it seems," she commented acerbically.

"Look, I never considered having a committed relationship or starting a family until I'd achieved my career goal targets because I never wanted a child of mine to miss out on anything—whether it be financially or emotionally. You want the same thing, right? For our child to have everything he or she needs to be happy, healthy and safe? Loving parents are part of that package. Perhaps we ought to consider being a couple."

"What, go steady, you mean?" she said with a gurgle of laughter.

"More than that. We should get married. Think

about it—it makes perfect sense. This is only a one-bedroom apartment, right? Where would you put the baby when it's born? Have you even thought about that? And what about work? Do you plan to be a stay-at-home mom or continue with your career?"

Sally put her glass down very slowly. "Kirk, we only just found out about this pregnancy today. We have plenty of time ahead of us for decision making. Let's not be rash."

"Rash? I don't think so. It's logical."

"I'm sorry, but it isn't logical to me in the least. We hardly know each other, and I'm not sure that I want to be married to you. I'm certainly not going to make a decision like that on such short acquaintance."

Kirk fought back the arguments that sprang to the tip of his tongue. It was clear she was feeling more than a little overwhelmed by his suggestion, which was entirely understandable. She needed time to think, and so did he. If he was going to campaign successfully to win Sally's hand, he would have to go about it carefully.

"At least think about it," he urged. "And talk to me—seriously, anything. Any questions, any problems, bring them to me and we'll solve them together."

"Oh, I'll be thinking about it," she admitted with a rueful shake of her head. "I imagine I'll be thinking about little else. By the way, I don't want anyone else to know about this just yet."

He nodded. The only person he would have shared

the news with would have been his mother, and with her gone he had no one else. No one else except the child now nestled inside the woman sitting opposite him. A feeling bloomed within his chest—pride tinged with a liberal dose of an emotion he'd had little enough experience with. Love. It was odd to think that he could love another being before it truly came into existence in the world, but he knew, without doubt, that he loved his child, and the intensity of the emotion shook him to his core.

Sally wasn't sure what was going through Kirk's mind, but if the determined look on his face was anything to go by, she was going to have some battles on her hands over the next few months. Probably over the next few years, she amended. He was a man used to having his way—it was inevitable that they were going to bump heads from time to time when it came to deciding what was best for the baby.

Her head swam. Discovering she was pregnant was shocking enough. Dealing with Kirk as her baby's father was another matter entirely—especially now that he seemed to believe they should get married.

Over the past couple of years, life had shown her that you had to reach for the things that mattered most to you. Had to fight for them. Her best friend from college, Angel, who'd turned out to be a secret European princess, had shown her how important it was to follow and fight for your dream.

Dissatisfied with a politically arranged betrothal based only on expedience with no affection attached,

Angel—or, Princess Mila, as she'd been officially known—had broken with tradition and done everything in her power to ensure she won her betrothed's heart, even at the risk of losing him altogether.

Just weeks ago, they'd celebrated the christening of their first child, a little boy who would become crown prince of Sylvain—and to Sally's eyes, when she'd visited to attend the ceremony, neither Angel nor King Thierry had ever looked happier or more fulfilled.

She wanted that. She wanted a man who would look at her the way King Thierry looked at Angel. There was no doubt in the world that Angel was his queen in every sense of the word. While Sally had always hoped to be a mother someday, she'd intended to start that stage of her life by finding the right man to be a husband and father first. Had planned to bring her child into a home already filled with love and trust. How could she have any of that with Kirk? She didn't love him—she barely knew him. And trust? Not a chance. The only positive traits she could assign to him were his appearance, his bedroom skills and the fact that he seemed to be a very capable boss. *Her* boss, in fact. And that added another layer of complication.

Sally wanted a life that was lived with purpose. One that yielded great results for others as well as for herself. She wanted to make a difference, and she ached to fulfill her potential. It's what she'd spent at least eight years of her life studying for and even more time interning at Harrison IT for. And yet despite her dreams, she continued to remain in the background. Knowing she was being held back by her phobia was one thing, but having a baby added a whole other layer to things.

Kirk had spoken of his career plans, but what would this do to her long-term goals? No matter what anyone said, life was very different for a woman in the workplace. That glass ceiling was still well and truly in place, and there were few women in the upper echelons of management. She'd hoped that one day, if she could overcome her phobia, she might earn a position up there. That the people she worked with would respect that she'd climbed her way up that corporate ladder, striving as hard as the rest of them.

No one would take her seriously if she was married to the vice president. Any advancement in her career would be looked upon as being won because of who she was, not what she brought to the role.

"Look," she started. "I've got a lot to think about, and you're right—I'm tired and I need an early night. Would you go, please?"

"You promise me you'll have something to eat?"

She gave him an are-you-serious look.

"Okay, okay," he said, holding up one hand. "Don't shoot me for caring. You have no idea what it was like to watch you crumple like that this morning."

He made it sound like he actually cared.

"I will have something to eat."

"I cook a mean omelet. If you have eggs, I could make it for you."

Her mouth watered. "Fine," she said, making a sudden decision. "I'm going to grab a shower. I'm not sure what's in the fridge, but go knock yourself out."

Maybe once he fed her, he'd stop hovering over her like some overprotective parent. She stopped in her tracks. But that's exactly what he was—a parent—and so was she. She shook her head, went through to her bathroom and quickly stripped off her work clothes. She looked at herself in the mirror.

"Nothing to see here," she murmured out loud.

But her hand settled on her lower belly, and for a moment she stopped to think about the changes that were happening inside. Changes that would force her to make monumental adjustments in her life. For a moment it all seemed too much and far too hard. But she reminded herself of what Kirk had said about wanting to be there every step of the way. She wasn't in this alone. Not by any means.

Did she have the strength to embark on this journey with him?

By the time she stepped out of the shower and dressed in a pair of yoga pants and a long-sleeved T-shirt, she was no closer to reaching a decision. A delicious aroma wafted from her kitchen, and she followed the scent to see what Kirk was up to.

"Perfect timing," he said, folding an omelet in the pan and sliding it onto a plate that already had a generous helping of diced fried potatoes, bacon bits and onions on one side.

"I had all these ingredients?" she asked, sliding into a chair at the breakfast bar.

"You can do a lot with just a few key things. When I was growing up, I often helped my mom in the kitchen. She taught me a lot."

Sally felt a pang for the boy he must have been. Her own upbringing had been so vastly different. They'd always had staff, including a cook, and as far as Sally could recall, her mother had never so much as baked a cookie her entire privileged life.

Kirk reached for a jar of salsa and ladled a little across her omelet before putting her plate down in front of her with a flourish. "There, now eat up before it gets cold."

She forked up a bit of omelet and closed her eyes in bliss as delicate flavors of herbs and cheese burst on her tongue.

"This is so good," she said. "Thank you. I hope you made one for yourself, too."

"I can get something later."

"Oh, please, you've given me far more than I can eat. At least help me with what I have here."

"How about I whip up another omelet and you can give me some of your potatoes."

"That sounds like a good idea."

It felt oddly normal to watch Kirk working in her kitchen. He moved with an elegant grace and confidence that she found all too appealing. *He withheld his true identity*, she reminded herself. *And he slept with you knowing exactly who you were.*

And now they had made a baby.

She was going to have to press him for an explanation about that night, especially if they were going to move forward together and most especially if she was even going to begin to seriously consider his proposal. But not now. Not tonight. Right at this moment she was struggling to make sense of what her next step would be and how on earth she was ever going to be able to tell her father that she was expecting Kirk's child.

Kirk took over cleanup duties when they'd finished their impromptu meal. Sally was too tired to argue the point by then. The food had given her a boost, but right now her bed was calling. Once he'd finished, she walked Kirk to the door.

"Thank you for dinner," she said softly.

"I enjoyed it. I…" He paused a moment as if debating whether or not to say what was on the tip of his tongue. "I enjoy being with you."

Sally didn't quite know how to react. He was good company and she felt drawn to him in a variety of ways, but there was so much about him that she didn't know—or trust. She reached for the door and opened it to let him out.

He was standing close, too close. The lure of his cologne mingled with the heat of his body and wrapped itself around her. She looked up at him and saw the way his pupils dilated as their gazes meshed. She wasn't sure who moved first, but one moment she was standing there with the door open, the next it was closed and her back was pressed against the wooden surface as his lips hungrily claimed hers.

Eight

She gave a small moan of surrender, and in the next moment he was lifting her as if she weighed nothing, the hard evidence of his arousal pressing against her sex, sending jolts of need through her body.

She wrapped her legs around his hips, pulling him tighter against her. His mouth was hungry and demanding, and she was equally voracious—meeting the questing probe of his tongue with her own, nipping at his lips. Through the cloud of need that gripped her, Sally became aware that she was no longer pressed against the door and Kirk was carrying her in the direction of her bedroom.

He lowered her to her bed and bent over her.

"I want to see you. All of you," he murmured even

as he peppered small kisses along her jaw and down the column of her throat.

She was at a loss for words. One minute they'd been saying goodbye and the next, here they were, tugging each other's clothing off as if they couldn't bear to wait another second before they were skin to skin again. Right now, the only thing that mattered was losing herself in his touch, in the sensations that rippled through her body with his every caress.

"Your skin—it's as soft as I remember," he said reverently, stroking her underneath her top.

"You remember touching my skin?" she asked on a breathless laugh.

"Among other things."

"Tell me about those things," she implored him.

And he did, in clear and graphic detail. Following up every word with a stroke of his tongue on her heated flesh, with the heat of his mouth through her bra as he teased her tightly drawn nipples into aching buds of need, and with the tangle of his fingers as they stroked and coaxed the slick flesh at her core. Her first orgasm rocketed through her body, taking her completely by surprise, but he took his time over coaxing her body to her second.

She continued to shiver in aftershocks of delight beneath the onslaught of his mouth as he traced her every curve. And when his head settled between her thighs, she nearly lifted off the bed as he gently drew the swollen, sensitive bud of her clitoris against his tongue. Her second climax left her weak and trembling against the sheets, and when he shifted slightly to slide on a condom, she laughed.

"Locking the stable door after the horse has bolted?" she teased, reaching for him as he hovered over her again.

"You could say that. Maybe it's just taking longer for the news to sink in than I thought it would."

Whatever she'd been about to say in reply fled her mind as he nudged his blunt tip against her entrance and slid deep within her. She rocked against him, meeting his movements—at first slow and languid and then speeding up as demand rose within them both again. This time, when she came, he tipped over the edge with her, and she held his powerful body as paroxysms of pleasure rocked them both.

Minutes later, exhausted, she slipped into sleep, unaware of the man who now cradled her sweetly in his arms.

Kirk lay there waiting for his heart rate to resemble something close to normal. If he didn't take care, *he'd* be the one needing a bed in the cardiac care unit. The dark humor sobered him up immediately. This was Orson Harrison's daughter he was sleeping with. And while the man was recovering nicely from his heart attack, he still wasn't back at full strength. He still needed Kirk to carry the load of the company for him. Finding out about the baby had thrown Kirk for a loop, but he couldn't allow it to make him forget all his other responsibilities.

He allowed his fingertips to trace small circles on

Sally's back as he listened to her deep gentle breathing. Somehow he had to disentangle himself from her warm, languid body and get dressed and get out of here. Put some distance between them so he could clear his head and do the job he was here to do.

While it was still possible that Sally was the leak that was passing information on to HTT's biggest competitor, he no longer wanted to believe that it could be her. Not the mother of his child. Not the daughter of the man he held in higher regard than any other man he'd ever known.

This pregnancy was a messy complication, but they'd work through it. Sally shifted against him, and Kirk found himself curving naturally to her. This wasn't the action of a man about to leave the woman lying next to him, he warned himself, and yet, try as he might, he couldn't find the impetus he needed to pull away. Perhaps just this once, he told himself, letting sleep tug him into its hold. It wasn't the cleverest thing in the world to remain in her bed, but for now it felt like the right thing.

It was still dark when he woke. Dawn wasn't far away. Beside him, Sally slept deeply, and he gently extricated himself from their intertwined limbs. His body protested, an early-morning erection telling him that leaving the bed was the last thing he should be thinking about. But he needed to get home to change before getting into the office for an early meeting. And he needed to examine his growing feelings for the woman still slumbering in the mussed-up sheets.

He quickly and quietly dressed in his shirt and trousers and, carrying his jacket and shoes in one hand, he made to leave the room.

Something made him look back and take one more look at Sally as she lay there, the sheet halfway down and exposing her back and the curve of a perfectly formed breast. It took all his self-restraint not to drop his things where he stood and move to take her back in his arms.

Work, he told himself. *Think of work.* He wanted to be in full possession of all his faculties by the time he and Sally crossed paths in the office today. As he left her building and walked toward his car, he saw a town car creep into the visitor parking area. He recognized the man at the wheel as the bodyguard he'd met last night. It made him think. One of Sally's security team could just as likely be the leak he needed to find and eradicate from HTT. He knew how easy it was to conduct a business call in the back of a car without considering the ears of the person driving.

Benton got out of the vehicle and looked across to where Kirk was parked. The man's eyes narrowed as he identified him. Taking the bull by the horns, Kirk walked toward him. He didn't want gossip about his relationship with Sally, such as it was, getting back to the office until she was ready for it to be made public.

"Good morning," he said to the bodyguard, extending a hand.

Benton's grasp was firm. Perhaps a little too firm, Kirk judged with an ironic lift of his brow.

"Morning, sir."

"I trust that Ms. Harrison's best interests are always at the forefront of your mind, Mr. Benton."

"Always, sir."

"Then I hope I can rely on you to keep the fact you saw me here this morning to yourself?"

The man hesitated a moment. "That depends, sir."

"On?"

"On whether or not *you* are in her best interests… sir."

Kirk nodded. "Fair comment. I will never do anything to hurt Ms. Harrison. You can rest assured on that score."

"Then we don't have anything to worry about, do we, sir?"

"No, we don't. Have a good day, Mr. Benton."

"Just Benton will do, sir."

Kirk nodded again and returned to his car. Somehow he didn't think that a bodyguard who took his duty to Sally so seriously could be a mole, but he'd have to check. Both Benton and whoever else ferried her about.

He looked up to Sally's apartment windows and saw the bedroom light come on. He needed to get going.

That evening, after work, Benton drew the car to a halt outside the front portico of her father's house. Sally thanked him and made her way to the door, where the housekeeper stood with a welcoming smile on her face.

"Good evening, Ms. Harrison. Mr. Harrison is in the library waiting for you."

"How is he today, Jennifer?"

"He's almost his old self, but we've had to remove all the saltshakers from the house."

Sally gave a rueful laugh. No matter what his cardiologist told him, her father still railed against his new dietary restrictions. "I'm so glad you have his best interests at heart. I don't know what we'd do without you all."

"It's our honor to work for Mr. Harrison. We're just glad he's recovering so well."

"Aren't we all?" Sally said with a heartfelt sigh.

She made her way to the library, where her father sat before an open fire nursing his one approved glass of red wine a day. He put down his drink when he saw her and rose to give her a welcoming hug. There was nothing quite like it in the world, Sally thought as she allowed her father's scents and strength to seep into her. And it still terrified her that she'd come so close to losing him.

"Hi, Dad. I hear you're giving the staff grief about your food again?" she said as they let each other go.

"Just keeping them on their toes," he said with a gruff laugh. "Can I pour you a glass of wine? This is a very nice pinot noir—you should try it."

"I—no, not today, thanks, Dad. I'll just stick with mineral water."

At some point she was going to have to tell her father why she wasn't drinking alcohol. She wasn't looking forward to the revelation, but she certainly wanted him to hear it from her before he had the chance to find out through anyone else. Especially after her fainting spell at work yesterday. Gosh, was it only yesterday? It already seemed a whole lot longer ago.

Her cheeks fired as she remembered exactly what had chased so much of yesterday's activity from her mind.

"Too hot in here?" her father asked, handing her a glass of water.

"No, no. It's fine. Lovely, in fact," she answered, flustered.

"Then what is it? What's bothering you?"

That was the trouble with being close to your parent, she admitted. They knew you too well and saw too much.

"A few things," she hedged.

"Is it work? I hear that Kirk has ruffled a few feathers. Glad to hear he's given your sustainability initiative the green light. It's about time we did more than just talk in circles about that."

He'd heard that already? Sally gave an internal groan. What else had he heard?

Knowing her father was expecting a reply, she managed to say, "Well, I always expected some pushback. You didn't seem so eager to embrace the idea, yourself."

"Couldn't be seen to be championing my own daughter, now could I. Had to make you work for what you wanted. I've always thought, if you're passionate enough about something, you'll make it work." Orson took a sip of his wine and put the glass back down beside him. "Now, tell me what you think about Kirk."

Sally felt the burn of embarrassment heat her from the inside out. Ah, yes, Kirk. That would be the man she'd slept with after turning down his proposal, after discovering she was pregnant with his baby. It sounded worse than the plot of a soap opera. She groaned to herself. Her father sat opposite her, clearly awaiting some kind of response from her.

"He seems to be very…focused."

Orson snorted. "He's good-looking, isn't he?"

"Dad!" she remonstrated.

"Focused." He snorted again. "The man looks as though he stepped off the front cover of *GQ* magazine, has a Mensa-rated IQ and you tell me he's *focused*. You're attracted to him, aren't you?"

"Dad, I don't think…" Sally let her voice trail off.

How did she tell him just how attractive she found Kirk? How he was so irresistible that the first night she saw him, she slept with him? That she'd done the same again last night?

Orson laughed. "I'm sorry, honey, can't help but tease you a little. You're so buttoned up these days. You can't blame your father for giving you a little prod. Besides, you can't argue the truth, can you?"

Sally chose to ignore his question and turned the conversation in another direction.

"Actually, now that you're better, could you please explain to me just why you brought him into Harrison IT? We were doing okay. We certainly didn't need to merge with anyone else, did we?"

And she certainly hadn't needed to *merge* with Kirk Tanner, but that hadn't stopped her from doing it again, that pesky little voice inconveniently reminded her.

Orson picked up his wineglass and swirled the ruby-colored liquid around the bowl, staring at it for a while before putting it back down.

"I guess, in part, you could call it guilt. Kirk's father, Frank, was my best friend in college. We started in business together. But what I didn't notice was that the man whose partying seemed harmless in college got in over his head when he partied hard in the real world, too. It got to the point where it took a lot of chemical help for him to get through the day. I didn't realize he was a drug addict until it was too late. By then he had a wife and son, and he was pretty resistant to help. Eventually he agreed to go to rehab, but he never got there. Instead he loaded up on drugs and took a dive off Deception Bridge."

He fell silent for a while, obviously lost in the pain of his memories. Eventually he drew in a deep breath and huffed it out again.

"I felt responsible. I should have been able to see the problem sooner, step in earlier, help him more."

"Dad, not everyone wants to be helped."

"I know that now, but back then I felt like it was all my fault. I did what I could to assist Sandy and Kirk when they relocated to California, and I set up a college fund for the boy. I've kept an eye on him.

What he's done pleases me. I guess, in the grand scheme of things, you could say he's where he'd have been all along if things had gone differently with his father. Merging with Tanner Enterprises was a logical move—gives us both more strength in an ever more competitive market."

Even though he'd given her a backstory of sorts, Sally had a feeling he was still holding something back. As it was, she was still hurt he'd had such an influence in Kirk's life and yet never shared any of that information with her.

"Marilyn called me just before you arrived. She tells me that Kirk took you to the doctor yesterday, that you collapsed or something during your presentation. Honey, you have to stop pushing yourself. You may never get over that public speaking thing, and if so, that's fine. But, that aside, tell me—you're all right?"

His pale blue eyes, the mirror of her own, looked concerned. While he might not see fit to include her in his business plans, he was still and always would be her dad, and she knew he loved and cared for her.

"Everything's fine, Dad. Nothing to worry about."

He looked at her with a piercing gaze. "What are you not telling me?"

She gave a gentle laugh. "I could ask you the same thing. Like why had I never heard of Kirk before the merger announcement. Don't you think that's something you might have shared with me at some stage? You've treated him like an absentee son."

An awful thought occurred to her. Could Kirk be

his son? But her father's perspicacity showed true to form.

"Don't be silly. You can turn that overactive imagination of yours off right now. There's no reason for the secrecy other than the fact that his mother wanted no reminders of her late husband or her life in Seattle in any way. While she reluctantly accepted financial help, that was where she drew the line. I had very little direct interaction with her or with Kirk. Your mother and I were friends with Sandy and Frank. We would have supported Sandy here, too, if she'd have let us."

Sally felt all the tension drain out of her in a sudden rush. Jennifer chose that minute to return to the library.

"Dinner is served in the small dining room, if you'd like to come through now."

Sally got up and tucked her arm in the crook of her dad's elbow, and together they walked to dinner.

"Dad, this place really is too big just for you. Have you ever thought of downsizing?"

"Why would I do that, honey? This house was your mother's pride and joy, and she loved every inch of it. She might not still be with us, but I feel her in every nook and cranny of the house and see her touch in every piece of furniture and art. Besides, I'd like to think that one day you might move back home and build your own family here."

Sally felt a clench in her chest. She should tell her dad about the baby, but how to bring it up? There was no way to dress up the fact that this child was the product of an unfortunate accident during a one-night stand. Granted, the man in question was already held in high regard by her father, but didn't that just complicate matters more?

Her father seated her at the table before taking his own place. Jennifer brought in the first course—smoked salmon fillets on a bed of lettuce and sliced avocado. Sally eyed the plate warily. She didn't know much yet about how to weather this pregnancy but she'd done a little research on foods she could and couldn't eat, and she knew that smoked or pickled fish was on the horribly extensive no list.

Orson noticed immediately that Sally only picked at the lettuce and avocado, pushing the salmon to the side of her plate.

"You're not going to eat that? I thought it was one of your favorites. You're not on some weird diet, or something, are you?"

She sighed. He was going to have to know sooner or later. "No, Dad. Not a diet. Actually, I have a bit of news for you."

"What's that? You're not going to tell me you're pregnant, are you?" He said it jokingly, but his face sobered when he saw Sally's expression.

"Well, that rather takes the wind out of my sails," she said softly.

"Really? You're making me a grandpa?" Orson's face lit up.

It wasn't the reaction she'd expected. After all, as far as he knew, she wasn't even in a relationship with anyone, and he'd always made his thoughts on the challenges of sole parenthood quite clear. It was probably another reason why he'd supported Sandy Tanner and Kirk the way he had.

"Apparently," she admitted ruefully.

"Was that the reason for your fainting spell at work yesterday?"

She nodded.

"So you managed the speaking part okay?"

What was wrong with him? Why wasn't he demanding to know who the father of his grandchild was? She nodded again.

"That's great news, honey! And a baby, too."

He leaned back in his chair and smiled beatifically.

"You're not bothered by that, Dad?" Sally had to ask because his lack of questions was driving her crazy. She'd expected a full inquisition. Had mentally prepared for one all day, knowing she wouldn't keep this secret from her father for long.

"Bothered by the baby? No, why should I be?"

"But don't you want to know—"

Her father leaned toward her and patted her on the hand. "It's okay, honey, I know where babies come from these days. I expect you got tired of waiting for Mr. Right and decided to go with one of those designer baby outfits. Of course, I'm sorry you didn't feel as though you could discuss it with me first but—"

Sally had been in the process of taking a drink of water and all but snorted it out her nose.

"Dad!"

"Well, it's not as if you have a regular guy, is it? I'd hoped you might meet someone special when you were at college, like I did with your mom, but that's neither here nor there. Looks like you'll be moving home sooner rather than later, huh?" He rubbed his hands with glee.

"Why would I do that?"

"Well, you don't have room in that cute little apartment of yours, do you?"

Sally rolled her eyes. What was it with everyone lately that they wanted to make all her decisions for her? First Kirk, now her dad—didn't anyone think she was capable of looking after herself?

"There's plenty of time to think about that, Dad. Besides, I can always get a bigger place of my own."

"But why on earth would you need to when we have all the room in the world here?"

It was about then that Sally noticed another place setting at the table.

"Were you expecting someone else?" she asked.

Just then, the chime of the front door echoed through the house.

"He's late, but he called ahead and said not to hold dinner."

"He?"

She didn't have to wait long to find out who *he* was. Within about thirty seconds of the door chime sounding, Jennifer showed Kirk into the dining room. Great, just what she needed.

"Good to see you, Kirk!" Orson said effusively, standing to shake Kirk's hand. "About time there was someone here who can share a celebratory champagne toast with me. I'm going to be a grandpa! Isn't that great news?"

Kirk looked at Sally, and she suddenly understood the expression "deer caught in the headlights."

"Dad, you know you shouldn't have more than your one glass of red wine a day. Doctor's orders, remember?" she cautioned, desperate to shift focus to something other than her pregnancy, especially since she and Kirk had agreed to keep it quiet for now.

"Just a half a glass isn't going to kill me. This is cause for celebration, whether you know who the daddy is or not."

"Know who the father is?" Kirk asked with a pointed look in her direction.

"I know exactly who the father is," Sally felt compelled to say.

"You do? Is it someone I know?" Orson asked, looking from Sally to Kirk and back again as he began to sense the tension between them.

"It is," Kirk said firmly and straightened his shoulders. "It's me. I'm the father."

Nine

"I didn't even realize you two knew each other that well," Orson said, sinking back into his chair.

"We don't," Sally said bluntly.

Kirk wasn't too pleased about the older man's color. Obviously hearing that his new business partner was the father of his impending grandchild had come as something of a shock. Just then, Jennifer came bustling through the door, bringing a serving of the appetizer for Kirk. He took a seat at the empty place setting and waited as the silence lengthened in the room. A silence Orson eventually broke.

"So what now?" he asked, reaching for his glass of water. "Are you going to marry the girl?"

"I have asked her to marry me."

"And?" Orson demanded, color slowly returning to his cheeks.

"The girl said no," Sally said, her tone revealing her annoyance at being discussed as if she was an accessory to the conversation.

"Why on earth did you say that?" Orson asked incredulously.

"It's still early," Kirk said smoothly. "We don't know each other that well yet, but I'd like to think that by the time the baby comes we'll be a great deal closer."

"You're obviously close enough to—"

"Dad—please! Can we not discuss this right now? We only found out yesterday ourselves, and we'd agreed to keep it quiet. I only told you because, well, you'd pretty much guessed already and I hate having secrets between us."

Kirk wasn't oblivious to Sally's silent censure toward her father. Those secrets included him, he had no doubt.

"It's only right that you told Orson," Kirk added.

"I don't need your approval, either," Sally said tightly.

"Now, honey, there's no need to be unpleasant," Orson interjected. "While I'm shocked, I have to admit that I'm relieved you have someone else in your corner. Becoming a parent is a big enough change in anyone's life. Doing it alone just makes things a whole lot harder than they need to be. What you need to realize is that you're more vulnerable now than you've probably ever been, and you have to make choices that are best for the baby, not just for yourself."

"I'm aware of that."

Kirk could see Sally didn't appreciate being talked down to. Orson apparently realized it, too.

"And now you're mad at me."

"Dad, I just wish you would let me be me sometimes. I'm a grown-up. I am capable of making decisions for myself."

Kirk had no doubt that last bit was directed at him, as well.

"Well, honey, I want you to think long and hard about the decisions you make now. I know your work is important to you. Mine always was to me, and over the years, I usually put it first. I have my regrets about that now."

"Regrets?" Sally asked, giving up all semblance of eating and pushing her plate to one side.

"Yes, I wasn't available enough to you while you were growing up, especially after your mother passed. I grew my business at the expense of my family, and while I can't turn back the clock on that, I can be there for you now. I hope you'll let me support you where I can."

Tears sprang to Sally's eyes, and Kirk felt something twist in his chest at being witness to this exchange between father and daughter. Far from offering his son this kind of support, Kirk's father hadn't even been able to hold himself together, gradually falling deeper and deeper into addiction. The memory and the scene before him only served to firm his resolve to be an active part of his child's life. No matter what transpired between him and Sally, he would be there for his son or daughter.

He hadn't managed to catch up with Sally in the office today. After returning to his new home before dawn and getting ready for work, he'd been caught up in meetings all day. One in particular had been distinctly disturbing, and it was part of the reason he'd agreed to come to dinner with Orson tonight.

It seemed Sally's project had been leaked to their main rival, who'd taken to the media already to advertise their willingness to implement sustainable workplaces throughout all DuBecTec offices, taking the thunder out of any similar announcements HTT might make in the future. Kirk's initial reaction had been to lay blame squarely with someone like Silas Rogers, who seemed to have some sort of grudge against Sally and might have taken action to keep her from getting credit for her ideas. But Kirk had enlisted the help of a forensic IT specialist, and it appeared that the information had been sent from Sally's own laptop.

The knowledge made him sick to his stomach. Not only because he'd spent last night with her, allowing his passion for her to overcome any sense of reason, but also because he realized he'd begun to develop feelings for Sally that went beyond the fact that he couldn't even be in the same room as her without wanting to touch her. Feelings that were now inextricably linked to the fact she was carrying his child—another complication he couldn't ignore.

His disappointment in discovering this proof that she'd been their leak all along was immeasurable. And, once the forensic specialist had found that link, it hadn't taken long for him to discover the others. All information going out had gone through Sally's device.

But mingled with his own feelings about the situation was the sadness of knowing Orson would be devastated. His own daughter behind the potential downfall of his pride and joy? They had to work fast to immobilize Sally and prevent her from doing any further damage. The fallout among her team would be another blow to the company. Those men and women would feel utterly cheated after all their hard work. Of course, HTT would carry on with implementing the plan—it made sense on so many levels Kirk was surprised it had taken this long. But they wouldn't be viewed as the leaders in their industry—they'd be the copycats. And that stuck in his craw like a particularly sharp fish bone.

He went through the motions with Orson, accepting a glass of champagne to toast the news of the baby, but his heart wasn't in the celebration and he could see Sally couldn't wait to be away from it, too. Dinner passed quickly, and Sally asked to be excused from sharing the dessert the housekeeper brought to the table—pleading weariness and the desire for an early night.

She'd blushed when she'd made her apologies. He knew exactly why she was so tired, but thankfully her father simply accepted her words at face value and, after exhorting Kirk to remain at the table, Orson saw his daughter to the front door, where her driver was waiting for her.

Kirk felt his stomach tie in knots as he considered what he was about to tell the older man on his return. There were many things the man needed to know— even if he wouldn't enjoy hearing any of them. Orson would be none too pleased to know that Kirk had deliberately hidden his identity from Sally that first night he'd met her, but Kirk knew he had to come clean and lay everything on the table—including the new evidence that had arisen today.

Last night had been one of the worst things he'd ever had to do in business. Seeing the devastation roll over Orson's face and knowing that he was the messenger responsible for putting it there hurt Kirk in ways he wouldn't have believed possible a few short years ago. But worse was yet to come. In light of the evidence, another special meeting of the board had been called this morning, and Orson had insisted on being in attendance.

Orson sat now at his desk and nodded to Kirk to make the phone call he was dreading.

He picked up the receiver and listened to the sound as Sally's office phone rang at the other end. The moment she answered, he spoke.

"Sally, would you be so good as to come to the boardroom at ten this morning? And I think it would be best if you brought a support person with you."

"A support person?" she repeated down the line. "What on earth for?"

"Please, I'll explain everything when you get there but you will need an advocate."

"Kirk, I don't like the sound of this," she insisted. "What's going on?"

"You'll get everything laid out at 10:00 a.m. Please be prompt."

He hung up before she could say anything else. Across the desk, Orson looked deeply unhappy.

"I'd never have believed she could do something like this to me, or to the company. Why? Why would she do it?"

That was the big question plaguing Kirk, too. Sally stood to gain little from the internal sabotage that had taken place. If her goal was to cause the company to fail, then she hadn't been very successful. While the firm had taken a hit in terms of new client work, they continued to operate strongly with their existing clientele. But growth was key to any firm's success, and she'd stymied that with her interference. The subsequent weakness now made them a prime candidate for a takeover bid. Had she been bribed or blackmailed by one of their competitors? What was really going on here?

He and Orson assembled with the board in the meeting room at nine thirty, and Orson quickly acquainted the board with the information about the leaks he'd gathered in the lead-up to the merger. Kirk then went on to explain the investigation he'd undertaken and the evidence the IT specialist had uncovered—in the briefest and most succinct terms possible. No one looked happy at the outcome, and all concurred with Kirk's suggestion of dealing with the perpetrator pending a fuller investigation. When the knock came at the door to announce Sally's arrival, there was a collective shuffling of papers and clearing of throats.

She looked shocked as she saw the full board assembled there, her face paling and reminding Kirk all too well of how she'd reacted during the video conference the morning after Orson's heart attack.

"Dad? What are you doing here?" she said. "What's this all about?"

"Take a seat, Sally," Orson answered with a voice heavy with gravitas.

Kirk noted Orson's PA, Marilyn Boswell, come in behind Sally and gestured to the two women to take a seat at the table. He saw Sally's hand shake as she reached for the glass of water in front of her and forced himself to quash the compassion that rose within him. He'd slept with this woman. Celebrated intimacies with her. Made a baby with her. And now she was the enemy. You'd have thought his experiences with his father would have taught him how to handle this feeling of betrayal.

"Thank you for coming this morning, Ms. Harrison, Ms. Boswell," he said in welcome.

Marilyn stared back at him fiercely before flicking her gaze to Orson. Her expression softened immeasurably. "What's this all about, Orson? We weren't expecting you back yet. What's going on?"

Orson looked across the table at his daughter, a wealth of sadness in his eyes. Kirk wished it could have been anyone else but Sally doing this to him. The betrayal that one of his own staff had sold out to the opposition was bad enough, but that it was his daughter?

Sally clenched her hands together in her lap to stop them from shaking. She felt as though something truly dreadful was about to happen. Her father hadn't mentioned anything about this meeting last night, but then again, he had been a little distracted by her news. When Kirk had told her to come to a meeting this morning and bring an advocate, to say she'd been stunned would be an understatement. This was their usual protocol when someone was being brought into a disciplinary discussion or, worse, being notified of redundancy. Why would either of those situations apply to her?

What if she actually had to speak in front of these people? Already she could feel her throat closing up and the trickle of perspiration that ran down her spine. Next to her, Marilyn reached over and placed her hand over Sally's.

"Everything will be okay, don't you worry. Your father won't let anything happen to you," the older woman whispered reassuringly.

Sally couldn't respond. Already her mouth had dried and her throat choked. Kirk rose to his feet and began to speak. He was a commanding presence in the room and everyone gave him their full attention. Or maybe it was that none of them wanted to make eye contact with her. Not even her father. The remains of the breakfast she'd eaten so hastily at her desk this morning, in deference to the growing child inside her, threatened to make a comeback.

The only one paying attention to her was Kirk, who seemed to be addressing her directly as he gave what he described as a summary of the information he'd shared with the board before her arrival. She listened with half an ear as Kirk listed a series of HIT initiatives that had been leaked to another company before the merger with Tanner Enterprises and explained the assignment that Orson had given him when he'd agreed to the merger. The lost contracts weren't news to her. After all, she'd also been shocked at how they had happened.

"The only logical conclusion we could come to is that there was someone internally working against the company. After an investigation, we believe we know exactly who that person is."

Sally looked around the room. All eyes were on her now. Realization dawned. They thought she was the leak?

No!

Ten

"Are you suggesting it's me? That I'm behind all this?"

The words felt like cotton wool in her mouth.

"Based on the evidence presented to us, yes. Would you like to respond to the allegation?" Kirk asked.

"Damn straight I would!" Anger seemed to overcome her fear of speaking in a group like this, and she shot to her feet. "How dare you accuse me of this? Dad? How could you believe him?"

"I'm sorry, honey. I didn't *want* to believe it, but the facts are all there. The information came from your laptop."

Sally felt the world tilt. Her laptop? The one she carried with her everywhere? The one with double password protection? She slowly sat back down, shaking her head.

"It wasn't me. Someone else must have accessed it."

"Are you saying you shared your passwords with someone else?" Kirk pressed.

"Of course I didn't. That's against company policy."

Giving access to her computer was almost as serious an offense as what they were accusing her of.

"I need a lawyer," she said, her voice starting to shake again as her rush of anger faded as quickly as it had happened and reality began to dawn. Whoever had framed her had done a thorough job. There was no way out of this without serious consequences.

"Yes, I believe you do," Kirk said firmly. "In the meantime, you will stand down from all duties and will forfeit all company property and passwords pending a full, externally run investigation."

"Stand down?"

"Standard operating procedure in a case like this," Marilyn said. "But don't worry. I'm sure everything will be just fine."

Sally begged to differ. Right now it seemed as though every facet of her life was in turmoil, and all of it tied back to the moment she'd met Kirk Tanner. Oh, yes, it was all too convenient, wasn't it? She remained seated at the table as one by one, the board members and her father and Marilyn left the room, leaving her alone with Kirk.

"This is all very convenient for you, isn't it?" she

said bitterly when the last person closed the door behind them.

"Convenient?" He shook his head. "It's anything but."

"Tell me, then. When you met me that night at the club, did you already suspect me of this?"

She had to know, even though hearing the truth from his lips would cause no end of hurt.

"Everyone was under suspicion. But—"

"But nothing. I was under suspicion, and you seduced me, knowing who I was. Did you think I'd let something slip in the heat of the moment? If so, you were wasting your time. I'm innocent. Someone, or several someones, have set me up. I already told you that it was hard for me to prove myself here. Obviously that goes deeper than I thought if an employee is prepared to go to these lengths to discredit me."

"And if that is the case, the investigation will show it and you'll be reinstated. In the interim, there'll be an announcement that you're taking a short medical leave."

Sally barked a humorless laugh. "And doesn't that fall right into your hands."

"What do you mean?" Kirk paused in collecting the papers that had been in front of him on the table.

"You already made it clear you want to take care of me and support me while I'm carrying your baby, and I refused you. Is this your way of ensuring you get your way? You're already proving yourself to be the son my father never had. How much more are you going to strip from me before you're done?" She wished she could unsay the words she'd uttered, but maybe now that they were out, she could face the truth of them. The truth that she'd never been good enough, articulate enough, strong enough to be the person her father had truly needed.

To her horror, she burst into tears. Kirk rushed to her side, and she shoved him away from her.

"Don't touch me. Don't. Ever. Touch. Me. Again."

She clumsily swiped at the tears on her cheeks. Kirk withdrew, but she could see the concern painted clearly on his face.

"You didn't answer my question," she said, her voice shaking with the effort it took to bring herself under control. "You already admitted you slept with me that first time, knowing who I was. Did you think it was me from the start? Was that why you didn't disclose who you were when you first met me? Because you suspected me of being the person responsible for undermining HIT—was that why you slept with me?"

He didn't say anything, and she could see her words had found their mark. It was a cruel reality to have to face that she'd been a target all along. For information and nothing else.

A shudder racked her body. And to think she'd even begun to consider what it would be like to be married to him. To build a family home together. What kind of a fool was she?

One who learned from the past, that's who.

"Sally, that night wasn't what I expected—hell, *you* weren't what I expected—"

"No. Stop." She held up her hand. "Don't bother. I get it. If you hadn't wanted information out of me, we'd never have met until the merger announcement."

"I didn't fake my attraction to you, Sally. From the minute you walked in that bar, you had my attention. But, yes, I realized that I'd seen you before, and it didn't take me long to figure out it was from the files your father had supplied me. I'd been going through all the staff profiles, trying to get a sense of the people I would be dealing with and, to be honest, trying to see who might have the means and a reason to be supplying our rival with sensitive information."

"Did my father suspect me?"

"No, he didn't, but he had to include you in the profiles because not to do so would be seen as showing bias. You understand that, don't you?"

She sighed heavily. "And now you think I'm it. So what now? You get security to escort me to my office to empty my drawers and then march me out of the building?"

"That won't be necessary."

She felt a glimmer of hope that she wasn't to be treated like a criminal, but then he continued.

"Marilyn will be instructed to remove your personal items from your office. As to the rest, including all your electronics and your cell phone, they'll be retained as part of the investigation."

Even though she knew she was innocent, the very thought of what was happening made her feel dirty somehow. Tainted. Would she ever be able to return and hold her head up high? Would her colleagues be able to look at her the same way? Trust her? Oh, sure. She knew that they were being told she was going on medical leave, but they were clever people. Her taking time off hard on the heels of the announcement by a competitor of an identical project to the one they'd touted to the senior management only two days ago? They'd put two and two together and links would be made.

She was ruined. Everything she'd yearned for, trained for and dreamed of had been torn from her by a traitor in this very building. She had to find some way to prove her innocence. Maybe then she could redeem herself in her father's eyes and in those of her peers.

"I see," she said with all the dignity she could muster. "Tell me, Kirk. Was I worth it?"

"Worth it?"

"The sacrifice of sleeping with me? Taking one for the team."

Before he could answer, she slammed her cell phone on the table in front of her, swept out of the boardroom and headed for the elevators. She pressed the down button and prayed for the swift arrival of a car to get her out of here. All her life she'd wanted to prove herself here—to be a valued member of the team—and now she was a pariah. She couldn't even begin to parse through her grief. And her dad? She'd seen the look on his face, seen the disappointment, the accusations, the questions. She hoped he would believe in her innocence once they'd had a chance to talk, but since Kirk so obviously already had her father's ear, what hope did she have of him believing her over Kirk?

The elevator in front of her pinged open, and she stepped into the car and hit the button for the lobby level. The doors began to slide closed but jerked back as a suited arm stopped them from closing. Kirk, of course.

"What? Did you forget to frisk me before I leave the building?" she baited him as he faced her and the doors closed behind him.

"Don't take this out on me, Sally. You know everything we've asked of you is standard practice while the investigation is being conducted."

"Don't be so pompous. You've lied to me from the moment you met me. Why not try being honest for a change?"

"You want honest?" he said tightly. "I'll give you honest. You caught my eye the second you arrived in the bar that night. I didn't recognize you immediately, but I couldn't take my eyes off you."

She snorted inelegantly. "I may be a little naive from time to time, but don't expect me to believe you on that one. There were any number of women, far more beautiful than me, in the bar that night."

"And yet I only had eyes for you."

The look she gave him was skeptical. "A little cliché, wouldn't you say?"

"Sally, stop trying to put up walls between us."

"Me?" She was incredulous now. "You're the one accusing me of corporate espionage!"

"Look, I feel sick to my stomach about this entire situation. We have to investigate further and we have to be seen to be dealing with this in the correct manner. I don't want to believe you're the culprit, but the evidence is too strong to suggest otherwise."

"How sweet of you to say so," she replied in a tone that made it quite clear she thought it anything but.

Sally held herself rigid as the doors opened to reveal the lobby. She had to get out of here. Out of the elevator, out of the building and out of Kirk's sphere. She started to walk, barely conscious of Kirk walking beside her.

"Sally!" he called as she strode out the front doors and onto the sidewalk.

She stopped and turned around. "You have no power over me out here. I'm just a regular person on the street right now. Remember? I don't answer to you or to anyone else."

"Where's Benton?"

"Right now, I don't know and I don't care. Maybe the decision has been made that I don't need a bodyguard anymore. I'd say my commercial value has dropped given this morning's revelations, wouldn't you? Don't worry your handsome little head about it."

Kirk took a step forward and took her by the arm. "You're still carrying my baby," he said coldly. "I have a duty to care for my child."

She closed her eyes briefly. Of course. The baby. There was always something or someone else that would take precedence over her, wasn't there. She opened her eyes and stared at his hand on her arm then up at his face. He wasn't holding her firmly, but he wasn't letting go, either. It drove it home to her that the life she thought she'd had was not her own. Never had been and likely now never would be.

Sally looked very deliberately down at his hand and then up to his face. He let her go. Turning on her heel, she walked briskly away from him and headed for home.

She'd been stuck at home for a week. The weather, in true Seattle fashion, had been gloomy and cold. Thanksgiving was only a week away, and Sally was finding it darn hard to be thankful for anything right now. The lawyer she'd spoken to had told her there was little they could do until charges were officially brought against her, if that indeed happened. In the meantime, she'd had dinner with her father a couple of times but the atmosphere between them was strained, to say the least. The good news was that he'd recovered enough to begin working again. He was doing half days at the office three times a week, and she had a suspicion he was also working a little from home. Not surprising, since his work had been his key focus all his life.

Medically he was hitting all his markers, and his cardiologist was pleased with his recovery. For that, at least, she was grateful.

Sally had caught up with her leisure reading and, wrapped up warm, had gone for several walks in the park over the past few days, but she itched to be able to use her mind to do more. Being inactive didn't suit her at all. And, all the time, it bugged her that whoever was truly behind the leaks from the office continued to work there. Obviously lying low for now.

She had spent a lot of her walking time thinking about the situation and what she could do to prove her innocence. Since her own access to the internet had been restricted by the confiscation of her equipment, she decided that she would have to use public means to conduct her own investigation. And that investigation would start with Kirk Tanner.

Last night she'd booked time for a computer at the Bellevue Library and when the cab dropped her off at the building this morning, she felt a frisson of excitement for the first time in days. She had a maximum session length of only two hours. She'd have to work fast.

Sally had always loved research and delving deeper into problems. Now she had something she really needed to get her teeth into. She started with Kirk. After all, wasn't he the epicenter of the quake that had shaken her life off its foundations?

It didn't take too much digging before she began to bring up information that related to Kirk's family. Thanks to the digitization of the local papers, there was plenty of information readily available about Frank Tanner, starting with a photo and article of him and her dad excitedly announcing their start-up IT company.

She stared at the photo of the younger version of her dad and a man who looked a lot like Kirk. The men's pride in their achievement was almost palpable. Sally sent the article to the printer and moved on to the next news story. This one was a lot less joyful. It described the arrest of a man under the influence of substances after police had been called to a domestic violence incident. The man was Frank Tanner.

A chill shivered down her spine as she read the brief report of his court appearance. A few years later there was another report—again with substance abuse, again with domestic violence. And then, finally, a brief report of Frank Tanner's death from a fall from Deception Bridge. The autopsy had reported that he had enough drugs in his system to cause multiple organ failure, even if the fall hadn't killed him.

Sally looked at the first picture she'd printed. Frank and her father had been so young then, so full of hopes and dreams for their future. Sally felt a pang of sympathy for Kirk, wondering what it must have been like for him to watch his home disintegrate, and at the same time grateful that she'd never have to truly know. Her father might have been focused on business, but at least he never raised a hand to anyone or ever let his family go without.

Discovering more details about Kirk's father's past went a long way toward explaining why his mother had been so determined to leave the area and make a new life for herself and her son in California. Sally could understand why Kirk was so driven, why he had a plan that he lived and worked by. His youth must have been so unsettled.

Her time was running out on the computer, so she quickly collated her printed pages and shoved them in her tote to read further at home. She knew her father had provided financial help to the Tanner family, including the fund that had seen Kirk through college. But was there more? Had Kirk somehow believed he had a rightful place at HIT? Had it been him who approached her father about merging their two companies? Had he possibly engineered a risk of potential takeover of her father's company to create an opening for himself where he felt he should have been all along?

Sally called her father that night and asked if she could come and visit with him over the weekend. When she arrived, he was still a little reserved with her, but as they sat together in front of the fireplace in his library, she decided to go at this situation head-on.

"Dad, do you really believe I'm responsible for the leaks at HTT?"

He looked at her as if he was shocked she would ask him such a thing. "I'd like to think not, honey. After all, why would you do such a thing? But Marilyn said you were frustrated at work, even though I never saw any evidence to support that. I always thought you'd bring any problems to me if you had them. It leaves me asking myself what you would hope to gain from such a thing."

Sally was a little taken aback. Marilyn had been telling her dad she wasn't happy at work? Sure, she'd often told the PA that she wanted to climb further up the corporate ladder, that it had been her goal to support her father in any way that she could. But she'd never expressed dissatisfaction to the extent that anyone could say she wasn't happy.

"Obviously I have nothing to gain," she said. "It wasn't me. I want you to believe that."

"And I want to believe it, too. However, what I think isn't the key here. We have to prove, beyond a shadow of a doubt, that it isn't you, don't we?"

She was heartened by his use of the term *we*, rather than the singular *you*.

"Tell me about the early days, Dad. About when you and Frank Tanner set HIT up. They must have been exciting times, yes?"

A gentle smile curved her father's lips. "They were very exciting times. The beginning of the boom times in information technology, and we were full of ideas and passion. Those were good years—challenging and exciting, difficult at times, but good nonetheless."

He fell silent and she knew he was thinking about his business partner's death.

"I learned a bit more about Frank Tanner's addiction, Dad. Why do you think he fell victim to it?"

Her father knotted his hands together and sighed heavily. "I don't really know. In college he was always the party guy, but he was so brilliant that it didn't hold him back. He never struggled to keep his grades up and always skated through exams without needing to crack open a reference book. I envied that about him. Everything I did, I did through sheer hard work."

Sally nodded. She was much the same.

Her father continued, "I guess he always put more pressure on himself to be more and do more than any other person. It was as if he was constantly trying to prove himself. Constantly striving for more and better than he'd done before. Money was tight for all of us when we started up, and we worked long hours. Frank even more than me. I guess he started depending on the drugs to keep himself sharp through the all-nighters. I could never figure out how he did it, but when I stop and look back, I realize he had to have been using something to boost himself.

"Anyway, by the time I realized he was dangerously hooked on drugs, it was too late. Not long after that, he was dead. As his friend I should have seen it, should have questioned him more closely. I should have recognized that he needed help, especially when things at home weren't so good between him and his wife."

"She always dropped the abuse charges, didn't she? Maybe, deep down, she still loved him and still hoped that he could change."

Orson looked at her. "I might have known you'd find that horrible history out."

"What can I say? I'm methodical, like my dad."

He gave her a smile, and he looked at her warmly. She'd missed this expression in his eyes since Kirk's accusations.

"What happened to Frank wasn't your fault, Dad,"

she said with deep conviction. "He was on a road to self-destruction long before you guys set up in business together. Even if you'd have noticed back then, do you honestly think you could have made a big difference? He had to want to change. If he couldn't do that for his family, he wouldn't have done it for you."

Her words were blunt, but they had the weight of truth behind them. She hoped her father would see that.

"I guess I know that deep down, but I still feel the loss of his friendship. When he died I had to help Sandy. She was a wreck, though she tried to hold it together for Kirk's sake. He was twelve when his dad died, a difficult age for a boy even without the additional test of having an addicted parent. I discussed it with your mother, who agreed we had to do whatever we could to help Sandy and Kirk start fresh. So we did."

Sally looked at her father. Going over the past like this obviously caused him pain, but she wasn't sorry she'd asked. She needed to understand the whole situation. She'd also hoped that perhaps learning more about the history of HIT might give her more insight into who was trying to hurt the company now. It distressed her that her father may still consider that she might be responsible for the leaks from HTT. Until she could remove every element of doubt, there would always be a question in his eyes whenever he looked at her. She couldn't live with that for the rest of her life.

"Dad, when did you begin to suspect there was a problem with information security at work?"

Orson looked a little uncomfortable and shifted in his chair. "It's been happening for about a year," he finally admitted.

Sally looked up in shock. About a year? That coincided with her appointment as head of her department.

Her father continued. "I did what I could but kept hitting blank walls when it came to trying to figure out who was behind it. That's when I turned to Kirk."

"Why him?" *Why not share your worries with me?* The silent plea echoed in her mind.

"I guess you're upset I never mentioned anything about him to you before," Orson commented with his usual acuity.

"Of course I am. I won't lie to you, Dad. It really hurt to discover him behind your desk the morning after your heart attack, especially after you'd presented me with the done deal at dinner the night before with no warning or prior notice."

"Well, in my defense, I did plan to be there with him. I didn't plan for my ticker to act up the way it did."

Sally got up from her chair and walked over to the fire, putting her hands out in front of her and letting the heat of the flames warm her skin.

"Why did you never tell me about your involvement with Kirk and his mom?"

"It wasn't something you needed to know," he said bluntly.

She thought about it awhile and was forced to concede he was probably right, except for one small fact—that he'd decided to bring Kirk in as his equal the moment the firm had been weakened. She decided to take a different tack with her questioning.

"Why do you think that someone has been sharing our details?"

Her father's response was heated. "Why does anyone do it? For money, of course. Why else would anyone betray the firm they work for? Someone has put their personal greed ahead of the needs of the company. Corporate espionage is a dreadful thing, and it creates weaknesses that allow others to gain leverage when it comes to hostile takeovers."

"Is that what was happening to us?"

Orson looked nonplussed for a moment, as if he'd let out more than he ought to have. Eventually he nodded.

"So there's been a threat of takeover," Sally mused out loud. "How do you know it wasn't Kirk behind it all along? Maybe he set it all up so he could come in as a white knight and suggest a merger."

"Kirk?" Her father sounded incredulous. "No. He'd never stoop that low. He's the kind of man who would come at a thing head-on. No subterfuge about that guy."

Wasn't there? Hadn't he withheld his identity from her the night they'd first met? It hurt and angered Sally, too, to realize that while her father refused to consider Kirk a suspect, he'd had no trouble believing it could be her.

"Besides, it was me that approached him from the get-go. I've kept an eye on him and his achievements ever since he and his mother left Seattle. I may have put him through college, but it's because of his own abilities that he's been able to really do something with his life. From the outset it was clear that he had his father's brilliance, but beyond that he had the sense to apply it where it would do him the most good. He had all of his father's best attributes, and none of the bad.

"To be totally honest with you, Sally, HIT needed Tanner Enterprises far more than the other way around. I was up front with him from the start. It was a risky move for Kirk to agree to the merger, but I needed him."

Sally could hear the honesty in her father's words, but that didn't stop the emptiness that echoed behind her breastbone that told her that no matter how bold she thought she could be, she would never be the kind of person who had the drive and hunger for success that Kirk so obviously had. If she had, wouldn't she have found a way to push past her phobia instead of hiding behind it?

She couldn't hold herself back any longer. She had to prove her innocence of the accusations leveled against her. And soon.

Eleven

Over the next couple of days, Sally spent hours trying to figure out who could be responsible for the leak. She covered her dining table with sheet after sheet of paper, many of them taped together with lines drawn between names and dates and points of data. On another sheet she wrote the lists of names and what people might stand to gain by such a thing.

After all her years at HIT, from intern to paid employee, she had gotten to know a great many of the staff within the various departments. She knew that because of the positive working environment and the benefits offered by the firm, staff retention was very high. She could understand the idea of a disgruntled employee wanting to punish their employer, but how could that apply here? Despite all the time she spent poring over everything, she still couldn't reach a solid conclusion.

Her days began to stretch out before her with boring regularity, and even a visit to her ob-gyn couldn't give her the lift she needed. Kirk had accompanied her, and the atmosphere between them had been strained. His presence at the appointment was just another confirmation of her links to a man who neither trusted her nor could be trusted. And yet, every time she thought of him, she still felt that tingle of desire ripple through her body.

A week after Thanksgiving, which she'd spent with her dad and Marilyn, she was struggling with a knitting pattern she'd decided to teach herself when the intercom from downstairs buzzed. She looked up in surprise, dropping yet another darn stitch from the apparently easy baby blanket she was attempting, at the sound. She certainly hadn't been expecting anyone, and when she heard Kirk's voice on the speaker she was unable to stop the rush of heat that flooded her body. Flustered and certainly not dressed for any kind of company, an imp of perversity wanted her to tell him to leave without hearing what he had to say, but she sucked in a deep breath and told him to come on up.

In the seconds she had to spare before he arrived, she dashed into the bathroom and quickly brushed her hair, tied it back into a ponytail and smoothed a little tinted moisturizer onto her face.

"There, that's better than a moment ago," she told

her reflection. "Shame you don't have time to do anything about the clothes."

Still, what was she worried about? This couldn't be a social call. A dread sense of foreboding in the pit of her stomach told her that this had to relate to her suspension.

Despite the fact she was expecting him, his sharp knock at her door made her jump.

"Just breathe," she admonished herself as she went to let him in.

She hadn't been prepared for the visceral shock of actually seeing him again. Dressed in sartorial corporate elegance, he filled the doorway with his presence, making her all too aware of the yoga pants, sweatshirt and slippers that had virtually become her uniform over the past couple of weeks. But it wasn't so much the way he was dressed that struck her—it was the hungry expression in his eyes as they roamed her from head to foot before coming back to settle on her face again.

"Hello," she said, annoyed to hear her voice break on the simple two-syllable word.

"You're looking well," Kirk replied. "May I come in?"

"Oh, of course," she answered, stepping aside to let him in the apartment.

As he moved past her, she tried to hold her breath. Tried not to inhale the scent that was so fundamentally his. Tried and failed miserably. Whatever cologne it was that he wore, it had to be heavily laden with pheromones, she decided as she closed the door and fought to bring herself under some semblance of control. Either that or she was simply helplessly, hopelessly, under his spell.

Maybe it was the latter, she pondered glumly as she offered him something to drink. Wouldn't that be just her luck.

"Coffee would be great, thanks."

"Take a seat. I'll only be a minute."

He sat down on the sofa where she'd been attempting to knit just a few minutes ago, and she saw him lean forward to pick up the printed pattern for the baby blanket.

"Nesting?" he commented, sounding amused as he picked up her knitting and tried to make sense of the jumble of yarn, comparing it to the picture in his other hand.

"Something like that. I needed to do something to keep me busy," she said a little defensively. "It's my first attempt."

It wasn't, in truth her first attempt at this blanket. In fact it was about her twelfth, but the project was very much her first foray into the craft of knitting, and as she ripped her successive attempts out yet again and rewound the yarn, she found herself missing her mother more and more. Her mom had loved to knit.

"You're braver than me," he said simply as he put everything back on the coffee table.

Sally made herself a cup of herbal tea and brought it through to the living room with Kirk's coffee. She put the mug down on a coaster in front of him then took a seat opposite, not trusting herself to sit too near. Maybe with a little distance between them she could ignore the way her body reacted to his presence and maybe her nostrils could take a break from wanting to drown in that scent that was so specifically him.

"Why are you here?" she asked bluntly, cupping her mug between her hands.

"I wanted to deliver you the news myself," Kirk said, giving her a penetrating look.

"News?"

"You've been exonerated of any wrongdoing."

Even though she knew all along that she was innocent, Sally couldn't hold back the tidal wave of relief that now threatened to swamp her. Her hands shook and hot tea spilled over her fingers as she leaned forward to put her mug on the table. Kirk jumped straight to his feet, a pristine white handkerchief in his hand, and he moved swiftly to mop her fingers dry.

She thrilled to his touch but fought back the sensation that unfurled through her as his strong, warm hands cupped hers. She tugged her hands free and swiftly stood, walking away to create some distance between them.

"I can't say I'm surprised," she said, fighting to make her voice sound firm when she was feeling anything but. "I told you it wasn't me."

"Your father told me the same thing," he said smoothly.

Sally briefly savored the evidence that her father

had supported her in this after all. "But you still felt there was room for doubt?"

Kirk ignored her question. "The forensic investigation of your devices showed that a false trail had been set up to look as though the data had been sent from your computer. At this stage, they still haven't been able to ascertain exactly who created that path. Obviously it was someone with a very strong knowledge of computer technology."

"Which, considering we're an information technology company, narrows it down to maybe ninety percent of the workforce at HTT," she said in a withering tone. "Do you plan to suspend everyone until you've figured out who it is?"

"That would be counterproductive," Kirk responded with a wry grin. "As I'm sure you know."

She looked at him, wishing that seeing him again didn't make her feel this way. Wishing even harder that none of this awfulness of suspicion and doubt lay between them and they could actually explore what it would be like to be a couple without any of the stigma that the investigation had left hanging like a dark cloud around her.

"I'm free to return to my work?" she asked.

"Tomorrow, if that's what you want."

"Of course that's what I want. I have a lot to catch up on."

"I thought you might say that." He reached into the laptop bag he'd brought and fished out her computer, her tablet and her smartphone. "Here, you'll need these."

She all but dived in to take them from him. She flicked on her phone and groaned out loud at the number of missed calls and the notification that her voice mail was full. It was going to take her hours to sift through everything. Still, at least she had her devices back.

She put her things on the table and looked Kirk in the eye. "Are you satisfied with the outcome? With my being cleared of involvement?"

He sighed deeply. "More than you probably realize, yes."

"I'm glad. I would hate to think you still suspected me."

He looked at her again. "Why is that, Sally?"

"Because, despite everything, we still are going to have to raise a child together."

Was it her imagination, or was there a shaft of disappointment visible in his aqua-colored gaze?

"I would like to think that we can handle this thing between us with civility, if nothing else," she continued.

"Civility." He nodded. "When I look at you, civility is the farthest thing from my mind."

His voice dropped a level, and Sally felt the intensity of his words as if they were a physical touch. She fought for control again, determined not to allow herself to fall victim to her confused feelings for this man.

"My father told me about your dad and why he asked you to join forces with him. What he couldn't tell me is why you agreed."

* * *

Here it was, his opportunity to begin to mend fences with Sally. It had been such a relief when she'd been cleared of wrongdoing that he had come straight here tonight instead of calling her into the office in the morning. His motives hadn't been entirely altruistic. He'd missed her and ached to see her again. He'd spent every day wondering what she'd be doing, how she was feeling and hoping like hell she was looking after herself properly.

She deserved his honesty now more than ever before.

"I had several reasons," he said carefully, looking directly into Sally's eyes. "One of which was the fact that I had always held your father in very high esteem. He owed my mother and me nothing, but when my dad died your father helped Mom and me get a fresh start—away from the memories that made my mom so miserable, away from the shame that she carried in her heart that she couldn't help her husband or prevent him from killing himself."

He looked at Sally, searching for recrimination or disgust in her eyes. Instead he only saw compassion. It gave him a ridiculous sense of hope. He took another deep breath.

"That sense of helplessness was one I struggled with, too. You see, the whole time I'd been growing up, it was with a kind of barter system where I'd convince myself that if I kept my room clean and tidy, my mom wouldn't cry that day or my dad wouldn't fly off into one of his temper rants. Or I'd convince myself that if I did well at school and got good grades, my dad would smile and play ball outside with me rather than lie on his bed shaking.

"It became vital to me to control everything around me, to do whatever it took to coax a smile from my mother's face, to keep my father calm when he was at home, to deflect the attention of the neighbors on the nights when everything turned to shit. And then to act like nothing had happened each time the police came and took Dad away. I learned that if you wanted things a particular way, you had to do certain things in repayment—that you had to earn any good thing that you wanted in your life. And yet, with your father, he didn't expect anything in return for aiding my mother and me. He just wanted to help."

Kirk looked at Sally, wondering if she could even begin to understand the depth of his gratitude to Orson for all he'd done.

"Dad has always had a compassionate heart," she replied. "I think it's helped him do so well, but he tempers it with drive and determination. He doesn't suffer fools gladly, and he won't tolerate injustice or laziness."

"Exactly. I actually used HIT as my business study in college—I guess you could say my family connection led me to being a little obsessed with understanding everything my father had been a part of before it all went so wrong. Through that, I grew even more respect for your father. In fact, I modeled my own business structure on what he'd done—and

I modeled myself on how he's lived. When he approached me and asked me if I'd consider merging Tanner Enterprises with HIT, I could see more than one benefit for both of us. Structurally, it was a solid, sensible decision that would benefit both companies. But personally…he said he needed me, and I finally had a way to pay him back for all the good he'd done for Mom and me over the years."

Sally looked at him, her eyes glistening with emotion. "Kirk, I'm so sorry your childhood was so awful. I wish it could have been different for you."

"I don't. Not anymore. It helped to shape me into the man I am now—it helped me know exactly what I want from life and where I want to be."

"Ah, yes," she said with a soft smile. "Your plan."

"Hey, don't laugh. Everyone needs a plan, right?"

Sharing this with Sally felt right. He felt as if a weight had lifted from him.

"So, what happens to HTT from here?" she asked. "Now that you know I'm not the leak?"

"We keep investigating," he answered in a matter-of-fact tone. "And we will find the perpetrator. It's a deliberate criminal act, and they must be held to account."

"And what happens now with *us*?" she asked unsteadily.

"What do you want to happen?"

"Kirk, I don't know how to cope with this. I don't know who I am with you." She felt lost, afraid to speak of her feelings, but she forced the words out. "You made me believe things about myself that first night we were together that gave me confidence and strength. When I found out who you were, all that confidence in myself shattered and made me doubt my attractiveness and appeal all over again.

"You see, I may have grown up with more than you did, and certainly without the uncertainty you had when your father was alive, but because of who I am and who my father is, there have always been expectations on me. Expectations I haven't always been able to fulfill. You've seen the worst of it, the fear of public speaking—"

"But you've made inroads on that, Sally. I saw you at that sustainability presentation. You were totally in control."

She smiled. "Well, not *totally* in control, but better than in the past, I'll accept that. Until I fainted, anyway."

"But even that wasn't you. It was your pregnancy, not your fear."

She nodded again. "Even so, I ended up delivering what everyone there expected me to deliver. Failure. It's something I've made rather a fine art of since my mother's funeral. I had written a poem for her. All I had to do was read it, but I couldn't. I choked. I couldn't even tell my mom goodbye the way I wanted to. Now, whenever I get up to speak to a group of more than two or three people, I'm back there in the chapel, standing there in front of all those expectant faces—disappointing all those people and failing my mother's memory."

Her voice choked up, and tears spilled on her

cheeks. "Even remembering it—" She shook her head helplessly. "It feels like it was yesterday. It never goes away."

Kirk was at a loss. He knew from Orson that Sally had had professional counseling to help her deal with her phobia—and that it had been unsuccessful. He reached for her hands, holding them firmly in his and drawing her to him until she was nestled against his chest. He felt her body shudder as a sob escaped from her rigid frame. He put his arms around her and stroked her back slowly, offering her comfort when words failed him. He felt her draw in a deep breath and then another.

"I've failed my dad, too. And that's the worst of it. I wanted to be his trusted, dependable right-hand man more than anything in my life. I pushed myself in college, I interned at HIT—I did everything I could to be an asset to him, rather than another disappointment. Oh, don't get me wrong, he's never made me feel as if I've let him down. In fact, I don't think he ever expected me to join him in the upper echelon at HIT. Sometimes I think nothing would have made him happier than if I'd just stayed at home and taken on my mother's old positions on the boards of the charities she supported. He's always told me he will support me in whatever I decide to do. But I wanted to support him, too."

"He values your input, Sally. Never think for a minute that he doesn't."

"But he doesn't turn to me. I'm not there for him the way I should be. At least not in his mind. When push came to shove and the company needed help, he turned to you."

Again, Kirk was lost for words. There really was nothing he could say in response to what was an absolute truth. Sally's father loved her. But he didn't see her as the strong, capable woman she truly was—the woman hidden behind her fears and insecurities. Somehow, he had to help Sally fight past her demons, to achieve the goals she'd set herself. He, more than anyone, understood how important those personal goals were.

Sally tried to pull away, and he reluctantly let her go. She sat up and dashed her hands over her cheeks, wiping away the remnants of her tears and visibly pulling herself together the way he had no doubt she'd done many times before.

"Listen to me blubbering on. It must be pregnancy hormones," she justified with a weak smile. "I hear they wreak havoc on a woman."

"Hey, you can blubber on me any time you need to," he said. "Sally, I don't want you to ever feel you're alone in any of this."

"This? The pregnancy or the fact that you suspected me of being the company mole?"

She said the words with flippancy, but he clearly heard the hurt beneath them.

"It's little excuse, but I had to follow procedure when the evidence pointed to you. I already knew you couldn't possibly be the leak."

"Well, it certainly didn't feel like you were sure I was innocent at the time."

"I'm sorry," he said frankly. "I'm sorry I wasn't honest with you when we met, and I'm sorry I put you through these past few weeks alone. I know it's little consolation, but I was massively relieved when it was proven, without doubt, that you were in the clear. It was also vital to the integrity of the investigation that we be seen to follow all the right procedures."

He winced. The words coming from his mouth were so formal, so precise and correct. They weren't the words he wanted to say at all. He wanted to tell her how much he'd missed her, ached for her—how much he wanted to hold her and show her how he felt about her.

"You're right, it is little consolation, but I'll take it. Which brings me back to my earlier question—where do we go from here?"

He knew exactly where he wanted to go. Right into her arms. For now, he hoped actions would speak louder than words. He reached a finger to her cheek and traced the curve of it.

"I know where I'd like us to go," he said softly.

Her pupils dilated. He leaned forward. Her lips parted, and her eyelids fluttered closed as he sought her mouth with his own. When their lips connected, he felt his body clench on a wave of need so strong it made him groan out loud. Sally's hands were at his shoulders, then her fingers were in his hair, holding him close as he deepened their kiss—as his tongue swept across her lips and he tasted her. Every nerve, every cell in his body leaped to demanding life, and he swept his hands beneath her sweatshirt, skimming over her smooth skin, relishing the feel of her. Wanting more, wanting her.

She arched toward him, and he tore his lips from hers to trace the line of her jaw with small kisses, then down the cord of her throat. He felt her shiver in response, felt her fingers tighten. He pushed the fabric of her top up, exposing her lace-clad breasts to his gaze. With one hand, he slipped one breast from its restraint. Her nipple was already a taut pink peak. He bent his head and caught the sensitive flesh between his lips, flicking the underside with his tongue and coaxing sweet sounds from her that drove him mad with need.

Kirk scooped her up into his arms and walked with her to the bedroom. After that, time blurred but sensation didn't as they rediscovered the physical joy they promised each other, and when pleasure peaked, it was the most natural thing in the world to fall asleep locked in each other's arms.

"Marry me."

Sally barely had her eyes open, and those two little words were echoing in her head.

"What?" Her voice was still thick with sleep.

"Marry me."

"Good morning to you, too," she said, rolling out of the bed and grabbing her robe from the back of a chair.

"I mean it, Sally. You can move in with me now—my house is huge and designed for a family. If you don't like it, I'll buy something else. We can create the nursery together. Plan for the future together. Travel to work together. It makes perfect sense."

Did it? Shouldn't a declaration of love come with a proposal of marriage? Shouldn't it sound better than being just the right thing to do?

"I'll think about it. I…I'm not sure I'm ready for marriage."

"Hey," he said, pushing up to a sitting position— and Sally had to avoid looking at him as the sheet dropped to just below his waist. "I didn't think I was ready, either, but we can make it work. We have a lot going for us."

"In bed, maybe," she admitted, tying the belt on her robe tightly at her waist. "But we still hardly know each other."

"We can learn about one another better if we're living together."

"You're persistent, aren't you," she said with an evasive laugh. "I need time. We don't have to rush. I said I'd think about it, and I will."

Kirk rose from the bed, the sheet falling away to expose his nakedness as he walked toward her and lifted her chin with one finger. His lips were persuasive as he kissed her, coaxing hers to open so he could explore her mouth more intimately.

"I'll be waiting for your answer," he said, his voice—and a very specific part of his anatomy— heavy with desire. "Shall I wash your back in the shower?"

And just like that she was putty in his hands.

Hands that were already at the sash of her robe, undoing the knot and pushing the silk from her shoulders. Hands that roamed her body, cupping her breasts and tweaking at her nipples until they were tight points that sent shivers through her body as his palms skimmed their hardness. Hands that moved lower and pressed against the other nub of sensitive flesh at the apex of her thighs until she was quivering with need.

Needless to say, they barely made it into work on time. Even though her hair was pulled back into its usual ponytail, it was still damp. Sally hoped no one would notice and jump to the right conclusion, especially as she and Kirk had been seen together.

As she walked through her floor, she was welcomed back by several members of her team, who appeared genuinely concerned for her. It was gratifying. She was a part of this, a part of these people and what they did here. But she wanted more than that. She wanted more, period. She wanted a sense of certainty that she was working to her full potential, that she was achieving something worthwhile for herself, on her own merits.

If she agreed to marry Kirk, wouldn't she simply be absorbed into the life he'd created for himself? How would she maintain her hard fought for identity? How could she expect her colleagues to treat her as an equal rather than as someone they had to watch themselves around? And then there was her goal of moving up the professional ladder. Who would believe she earned a promotion when she had things nicely sewn up between her father and Kirk?

On a more personal level, Kirk had admitted modeling himself on her father, both professionally and personally. She already had one overprotective father in her life—she didn't need another person sheltering her constantly. When—if, she corrected herself firmly—she married, she wanted to be treated as an equal by her partner.

Kirk had already made it more than clear that he wanted to be her protector and provider. That sounded to her as if what she brought into a marriage didn't even rate a consideration on his revised grand plan. And, when it came to working together, based on Kirk's standing within HTT and his grasp of what the company offered and how they could remain current and relevant into the future, his knowledge and experience far exceeded her own.

Doubts flew at her from all directions. Maybe she never really would be any better than who she'd always been—the woman on the eighth floor who stayed in the background and allowed others to get the credit for her ideas.

Over the course of the day, as she caught herself back up on her projects, she found her mind wandering backward and forward until she was almost dizzy with it all.

As she sat down in her office to the lunch Kirk had packed for her before they'd hurriedly left her apartment, she forced herself to reevaluate her goals. After a great deal of deliberation, she had to recognize that, no matter what, she wanted to be a part of Harrison Tanner Tech now and in the future.

When Benton took her home that Friday evening, she was still in turmoil. Over the weekend, she spent time making a list of all the reasons why it would be good to marry Kirk Then, she made a list of why it wouldn't work.

"No matter which way you look at it, great sex does not equate to a great marriage," she said out loud once she was done. "And great sex does not equate to lifelong happiness, either."

By the time she went to bed on Sunday evening, she felt sure she'd reached her decision. Now it was just a matter of telling Kirk.

Twelve

Kirk had been in the office since five this morning. Staying one step ahead of the mole was a challenge he enjoyed getting his teeth into. The only thing he'd enjoy more would be unmasking the traitor and seeing them punished to the fullest extent of the law.

In the meantime, the company was running smoothly and the merger activities were fully on track. This week was shaping up well, and he was relieved that Orson would be back in the office full-time starting today. The man's recovery had been steady, and he'd been itching to get back to his desk full-time.

Kirk paused for a moment and considered the talk he'd had with Orson last night. Orson had continued to express his approval of Kirk marrying Sally. He was old-fashioned enough to want to see his grandchild born in wedlock, but he'd cautioned Kirk that while Sally appeared to be soft and gentle, she had a core of steel and a determined independence that didn't waver once she had her mind made up on anything.

He was heartened her father saw that in her but wondered if Orson had ever expressed any admiration for those traits to Sally's face. It might have gone some way toward helping her beyond her phobia if she realized that her father wasn't waiting for her to fail in everything she did—he was actually waiting for her to succeed. Of course, maybe she knew that all along. Maybe that was, in itself, as much of a yoke around her slender shoulders as anything else.

He felt a buzz of excitement at the idea of being married to Sally, of being a couple. Of waking to her each morning, of spending free time together and looking forward to the birth of their child. His son or daughter's life would be so vastly different from his own. And his wife wouldn't experience any of the suffering his father had put his mother through. Sally would never have to fear a fist raised against her in frustration or anger, and his child would grow up secure in the knowledge that their father was there for them every step of the way. There'd be no trade-off. No coercion. There would be love and stability and all the things Kirk had dreamed of as he'd made his plans for his future all those years ago.

A sound at his door made him look up. As if thinking about Sally had caused her to materialize, there she was. Kirk felt a now-familiar buzz of excitement as he saw her standing there. He'd seen Sally wear many different faces and in today's choice of a black tailored pantsuit with a pale gray patterned blouse underneath, she looked very serious indeed. As he rose and walked around his desk to greet her, he wondered if she wore one of those slinky camisoles beneath the blouse. His hands itched to find out.

"Good morning," he said, bending to kiss her.

She accepted his greeting but withdrew from his embrace quickly.

"Kirk, have you got some time to talk?" she said without preamble.

"Sure, for you, always."

He gestured for her to take a seat and he took the guest chair angled next to hers. As he did so, he studied her face carefully—searching for any telltale signs of tiredness or strain. She was a hard worker, harder than many here, and she needed reminders every now and then to put her needs before the needs of the company.

"I missed you over the weekend," he said.

She'd made it clear to him on Friday that she'd wanted space—time to think about them—so he'd given it to her. Now he wondered if that had been the right move. Her expression was hard to read as she looked up at him, the pupils in her eyes flaring briefly at his words. Did her body clench on a tug of desire the way his did right now? Had she spent the weekend reliving their lovemaking on Thursday night? She averted her gaze and shifted in her seat.

"What did you need to talk about?" he coaxed.

"I've reached a decision about your proposal."

He felt a burst of anticipation. "When can we start making plans?"

"I don't want to marry you."

What? "I see," he said slowly.

But he didn't see at all. When they'd come to the office together on Friday morning, it had felt so right, so natural. As if they'd been together forever and would be in the future, too. He searched her face for some indication of what she was thinking and watched as she moistened her lips and swallowed a couple of times, as if her mouth was suddenly dry. He got up and poured a glass of water from the decanter on his desk and passed it to her.

"Thank you," she said, taking a brief sip and putting the glass back down on his desk. "I didn't see the point in keeping you waiting on my answer. So, if there's nothing else we need to discuss, I'll get to work."

She got up from the chair and started for the door.

"Hold on a minute."

She froze midturn. "Yes?"

"I thought we were a little closer than that. Can you at least tell me why? Are you sure you've thought this through?"

"Since the first time you asked me, I've thought of little else. We don't live in the Dark Ages. Having a baby together is not enough reason to marry. We can coparent just as effectively while living our separate lives. I don't see why this—" her hand settled briefly on her lower belly "—should change anything."

Her voice grew tighter with each word. If he didn't know better, he'd have thought she was on the verge of a full-blown panic attack. But didn't that only happen when she had to speak to a group? Unless, of course, she was so emotionally wrought by the idea of turning him down that she was working herself up.

"Take a breath, Sally," he urged her.

"I'm fine," she said testily. "I'm perfectly capable of looking after myself. Look, I knew it wouldn't be easy to tell you my decision, and I suspected you wouldn't be happy about it. I just would like you to respect my choice and let us move on."

"You're right, I'm not happy about it," he said, trying to rein in his frustration and disappointment. "I didn't just ask you to marry me for convenience's sake, or because of how things look. I want to be a daily, active part of my son or daughter's life. I want to ensure that he or she doesn't miss out on the bond between father and child the way I missed out with my own father."

She closed her eyes briefly, and he saw her chest rise and fall on a deep breath. When she spoke, she sounded calm, but he could see the tension in her eyes and etched around her mouth.

"We can work to make sure that our kid knows we're always going to both be there for them. But that doesn't mean we have to get married or even live together—a shared custody arrangement will work perfectly well in our situation, just as it does for people all over the world. Seriously, Kirk, being married is no guarantee of a happy home when the two people involved don't love one another—it isn't even a guarantee when they do!"

Her voice rose on the last sentence, and he watched as she visibly paused to drag in a breath and assume a calmer attitude. "Look, I understand how you feel, but remember, you are not your father. You're not a drug addict. You're not going to let down this child, or any other child you might have in the future. It's not in your nature. I believe you'll be a good father, and I'm happy for you to be fully involved in your child's life. I just don't want to marry you. Please, will you respect my decision?"

There was a quiver in her voice that betrayed her rigid posture. If he was a lesser type of man, he'd push her now, try to persuade her otherwise. Use all the ammunition he could think of to try to get her to change her mind. But despite the desire to do so, he realized that if he pushed her too hard, he'd probably only succeed in pushing her away for good. He clenched his hands and then forced himself to relax, unfurling his fingers one by one. Decent men didn't give in to emotion like this. Decent men didn't bully or threaten so they could get their way.

"I do respect your decision," Kirk said heavily. "But I would beg you not to close the door on the idea entirely. Please allow me the opportunity to try to get you to change your mind."

"No. Please don't." Her voice was firm again and she was very much back in control. "In fact, I think it would be best if we confine our interactions to work-related matters only."

"You can't be serious. What about the baby?"

He couldn't help himself. The words just escaped. Was she truly closing the door on everything between them? Everything they'd shared?

"I will keep you apprised of my ob-gyn appointments and of course you can come along with me to those, but everything else—" she waved her hands in front of her "—stops now."

Kirk felt a muscle working at the side of his jaw, and he slowly counted to ten, forcing himself to relax. Then he nodded.

"If that's what you want."

"It is. Thank you."

He stood there, overwhelmed by disappointment and frustration as she walked away. This wasn't how he'd imagined this panning out at all. Sometimes, it seemed that no matter how well you planned things, it all just fell apart anyway.

By the time she got home, Sally couldn't remember how she'd gotten through her workday. From the moment she'd left Kirk's office, it seemed that everyone had wanted a piece of her and her time. The first of the new hybrid cars for the fleet were ready for pickup, and she'd had to coordinate the coverage with the managers involved and the PR team so when the next company newsletter went out it did so with the appropriate fanfare. There had been no point in making a media announcement. Not when DuBecTec had already stolen the wind from their sails.

Sally slumped down on her sofa, weariness pulling at every part of her body. All she wanted to do right now was take a nap. In fact, a nap sounded like a great idea, she decided as she swung her feet up onto the sofa and leaned back against the pillows she had stacked at one end. She'd no sooner closed her eyes than her cell phone rang. With a groan she struggled upright and dug her phone out of her handbag.

Kirk's number showed across her screen. She debated rejecting the call but then sighed and accepted it.

"Hello?"

"I just wanted to give you a heads-up. The media have gotten wind of the fact that you're pregnant, and that it's my baby."

All weariness fled in an instant. "What? How? Who?"

"That's what I'm going to find out," he said grimly. "But I wanted you to be prepared."

"But we agreed not to tell anyone. I'm not even showing yet. How could something like this have happened?"

Was this some ploy of Kirk's to try to get her to agree to marry him after all?

"The only other person we told is your father and I doubt he's responsible, but you can rest assured that I will be asking him."

With a promise to get back to her the moment he

had any further news, and an admonition to screen her phone calls to avoid being badgered by the tabloid press, he severed the call.

Sally stood where she was, trapped in her worst nightmare. Now it didn't matter what she did anymore. Everyone at work would know. There'd be sly looks and innuendo and, no doubt, outright questions, as well. She'd hoped to have time to manage the situation. After all, she was still getting used to the whole idea herself.

Over the last few weeks, whoever it was that had been leaking information had held back. Oh, sure, the company had still faced some media criticism. There'd been the occasional aspersion about her father's illness in the media—the rhetorical questions about whether or not HTT's dynamic leader would remain as much of a power broker as he'd been in the past—but with Kirk's strong hand at the tiller and his no-nonsense leadership style while her father returned to full strength, those questions had faded as quickly as they'd arisen. But this was a personal attack against her and against her right to privacy. She felt violated and sick to her stomach.

She had to do something. But what? Attempting to discover who their problem was by using logic hadn't worked. So what did that leave? Her mind reached for something that she felt she should know, but everything came up blank.

Her landline began to ring. No one she knew actually used it. Even her dad used her cell number. She took a look at the caller ID but didn't recognize the number and switched the phone through to her voice mail.

Sally went to take a shower and change for an early night. She was no sooner out of the bathroom than the doorman buzzed from downstairs. Apparently there was a TV crew from a local morning show wanting to speak to her. Sally shook her head in disbelief. Aside from the time when she'd almost been kidnapped as a child, she'd only rarely been deemed newsworthy. After all, it was hardly as if she held the same kind of profile as her friend Angel, and Orson had actively avoided letting his family be exposed to the limelight of what he called pseudo celebrity. "I'd rather our family be judged on our achievements and what we do for others than by whose clothes we wear or what we were seen doing," he always said.

With a few tersely chosen words, Sally asked the doorman to ensure that she wasn't disturbed by the TV team or by anyone else not on her visitor list. She walked over to her windows and looked down at the parking lot. A second TV crew pulled into the lot. The onslaught had begun.

Thirteen

Thankfully, by the next morning, the gossip news focus had moved to the latest public celebrity melt-down and Sally's pregnancy had been relegated to a footnote. That said, when she was ready to leave her apartment for work, she discovered there were two bodyguards assigned to her—one to remain with the car at all times, the other to escort her inside and ensure she wasn't harassed by anyone. She was surprised to learn that the additional man had been ordered by Kirk, but she wasn't about to complain. She had no wish to discover that her car had been bugged or to be ambushed by anyone with a microphone.

She had planned to have lunch with Marilyn today and was looking forward to catching up with her. Everyone had been working so hard lately that it felt like forever since they'd had a good talk. The morning went by quickly, and the photo shoot for the new cars and their assigned drivers went according to plan. Sally was beginning to feel like she had a handle on things. At one o'clock she went down to the lobby to wait for Marilyn, who was just a few minutes late.

Sally kissed the older woman on the cheek and gave her a warm smile when she arrived. Shadowed by Sally's bodyguard, they walked a block to their favorite Italian restaurant for lunch and were shown to their regular table.

"So, tell me," Sally asked after the waiter had poured their water and given them menus to peruse. "How are things in the ivory tower?"

Marilyn smiled a little at the moniker given to the executive floor at the top of the building. "Busy. Mr. Tanner has yet to appoint a PA of his own, which doubles my workload."

"Have you asked for an assistant? I'm sure Dad—"

"Oh, I don't want to worry your father about something as ridiculous as that. I do work a few extra hours now, but it's nothing I can't handle. I guess I should consider myself lucky. At an age when most of my peers are settling down and enjoying their grandchildren, at least I still have a rewarding career."

Did Sally imagine it, but was there a tinge of regret, or possibly even envy, in Marilyn's tone?

"I'm sure Dad wouldn't see it as a worry, Marilyn—you know you can talk to him about anything. After all, you've worked for him for how long now?"

Marilyn's face softened. "Thirty years next week."

"Wow, that's got to be some kind of record."

"Your father and I are the only original staff left. I keep telling him it's time to pass the reins on to someone else. For him to slow down and actually enjoy the rest of his life. For us both to retire." Her mouth firmed into a straight line, and her eyes grew hard. "But you know your father—work comes first, last and always with him. I would have thought with this latest business with the leaks to competitors, and then with his heart attack, that he would have learned his lesson about slowing down—but oh, no. Not him."

It was the first time Sally had heard bitterness in the other woman's voice when talking about Orson, and it came as surprise. Normally Marilyn would stand no criticism of her boss from anyone. To hear it from her own lips was definitely something new. Maybe it was just the extra workload she had now, supporting two senior managers, that had put Marilyn in a sour mood. Even so, Sally felt she needed to defend her father.

"He's always tried to make time for family—and HIT has always been his other baby. I don't think you should be too harsh on him."

"You know I care about your father. I only want what's best for him. It would be nice if he'd just stop focusing on work with that tunnel vision of his and look around him once in a while. Anyway, that brings me to something that's been bothering me awhile. When were you going to tell me about the baby, Sally?"

Sally swallowed uncomfortably. "I didn't want

to make a fuss at work, Marilyn. I'm sure you understand why, especially given how hard I've had to work to earn any respect there."

"But I'm not just *anyone*, am I? I thought we were closer than that."

"And we are," Sally hastened to reassure her. Marilyn looked truly upset that she hadn't been told, and, in hindsight, perhaps Sally should have included her in the news, but she'd had her reasons for wanting privacy, and they hadn't changed. "I'm really sorry, Marilyn. I don't know what else to say."

The older woman sniffed and reached in her handbag for a tissue and dabbed at her nose. "Apology accepted. Now, what are you having today? Your usual chicken fettuccine?"

Sally hesitated before closing her menu. "Yes, I think so."

Marilyn placed their orders and the food was delivered soon after, but Sally found herself just toying with her fork and pushing pasta from one side of her plate to the other. It wasn't that she wasn't hungry, but she was still unsettled by how Marilyn had spoken about Orson. She'd never heard the other woman make a criticism of her father before. Ever. To hear it now had struck a discordant note, and it got her to wondering.

Marilyn was privy to pretty much everything that went over Orson's desk. Given her current disenchantment, could she be the leak Kirk and Orson were looking for? She was the last person anyone would suspect, given her long service and well-documented loyalty to Orson. Was it even possible that she'd do something so potentially damaging to the company? How on earth would she benefit from something like that?

The questions continued to play in the back of Sally's mind over the next day and a half until she couldn't keep her concerns to herself any longer. She had to talk to someone about it. She called her dad at home and asked if she could come over.

Jennifer let her in the door as she arrived.

"Dad in the library?" Sally asked as she stepped inside.

"Where else is he at this time of evening?" the housekeeper answered with a smile. "Mr. Tanner is with him."

Sally hesitated midstep. Her dad hadn't mentioned anything about Kirk being over when she'd called. Maybe he hadn't wanted to put her off coming. She'd already told him that she wasn't planning to see any more of Kirk outside the office and that she'd turned down his proposal. Her father had expressed his disappointment, stating that he firmly believed a child's parents ought to be married. Without pointing out the obvious—that his stance on the matter was archaic at best—Sally had made her feelings on the subject completely clear, and he'd eventually agreed to abide by her wishes.

She'd barely seen Kirk in the office over the past few days. And she'd kept telling herself that was just the way she liked it. Regrettably, her self begged to differ. The thought of seeing him now made her pulse flutter and her skin feel hypersensitive beneath her clothes. *You can do this*, she told herself. She could talk to him and her father in a perfectly rational and businesslike manner without allowing her body's urges to overtake her reason.

"Thanks," she said to the housekeeper. "I'll let myself in."

"Can I get you something?"

"No, I'll be fine, thank you."

The idea of eating held no appeal. She already felt sick to her stomach over what she suspected. Maybe she was completely off track with it, but what if she wasn't? It would be good to have the benefit of someone else's opinion.

Her father and Kirk rose from the wing chairs by the fireplace as she entered the library. She crossed the room and kissed her father, nodding only briefly to Kirk.

"It was an unexpected, but lovely surprise to get your call this evening," Orson said when they'd all settled down again.

"It may not be so lovely when you hear what I came to say," Sally replied, smoothing her skirt over her thighs.

She stopped the instant she realized that the movement had attracted Kirk's attention. Her gaze flicked up to his face, and she saw the flare of lust in his eyes before he masked it. Lust was all very well and good, she told herself, but it wasn't love, and unless he could offer her that as well, she had to hold firm.

"That sounds ominous," Kirk observed.

"I could be completely wrong, but I think I might have uncovered the leak."

Both men sat upright, all semblance of relaxation gone in an instant.

"Who?"

"You have?"

Their responses tumbled over each other, and Sally put her hand up and looked directly at her father.

"Dad, you're not going to want to believe this, but I think Marilyn is behind it all."

"Marilyn? What? She's worked for me since before you were born. Heck, I've known her longer than I even knew your mother."

A shaft of understanding pierced Sally's mind. Was that an explanation for Marilyn's behavior? She'd said she cared for him, but was she in love with Orson? Had she been all along? Was that why she wanted him to slow down?

"Think about it, Dad. Who else had access to the information that's been spread? Even the news of the baby. No one else aside from the three of us knew at HTT. Unless you told Marilyn."

Orson shifted uncomfortably in his chair and puffed out his cheeks. "Well, I might have told her that I was looking forward to being a grandfather. She may have put two and two together from that. And as for linking you and Kirk together, she's very astute, and someone would have to be deaf, dumb and blind not to see the way you two look at each other."

Sally stiffened in shock. They would? She looked over to Kirk, who appeared equally shocked. He rubbed a hand over his face and leaned forward, elbows on knees.

"Sally, what brought you to this conclusion?"

Of course he wanted proof. As would she in the same position, but somehow it rankled that he was the one asking her, not her father.

"It was a few of the things she said to me over lunch the other day." Sally repeated them for the men. "There was a tone to her voice, a hardness that I hadn't heard in her before. She sounded really fed up. Bitter. Angry. Plus, she was the one to cast doubt on me, telling Dad that I told her I was frustrated with my job—which is not true."

"We'll have to interview her," Kirk said to Orson. "Test the waters without making an outright accusation. We'll need to be careful. We don't want her suing us for defamation."

"Oh, Marilyn wouldn't do that," Orson protested.

"If she's behind the leak of information, then she's already shown she's willing to hurt the company. I tell you what. I'll do a little investigating of my own. Have my forensic specialist delve a little deeper. If she is responsible, she's very, very good at hiding it. It might not be so easy to prove."

Sally fidgeted in her chair. She felt terrible for believing that the culprit could be Marilyn, but if she was their leak, she had to be stopped before she did irreparable damage to the company. Each information release had undermined HTT's integrity just that little bit more. The loss of new business had been felt, and if existing clients began to doubt the safety of their information and started to withdraw from HTT, it wouldn't take long before the company truly began to crumble.

"Should I tell her to take some days off?" Orson asked Kirk. "She's due for some time, and she's been working long hours lately."

"No, I think that would tip her off that we suspect her. Better to just keep things going as normal."

After a brief discussion about their plan of attack, Sally stood to leave.

"It's late and I'm tired. I'll be heading home unless there's anything else you need me for?"

Kirk stood, too. "I'll take you home. It's time I headed off, too."

"That's not necessary. I have my driver and my guard."

"Please, I'd like to talk."

"I'll tell Jennifer to let your men go," Orson said, getting up and going to the door. "And I'll see you two at work."

He was gone, leaving them alone together. Sally bristled at Kirk's nearness. She grabbed her handbag and headed toward the door, but Kirk beat her to it, holding the door open for her as she went through.

The scent of him tantalized and teased her. Reminding her of what she was missing out on, of what was right there, hers for the taking if she wanted it.

And she did want him. But what she really wanted was more than he seemed willing to give. Love, forever, the whole bundle. And he hadn't offered her that.

"Sally, slow down a sec," Kirk called as she strode out down the corridor to the front door.

He drew level with her, and she gave him a querying look.

"In such a hurry?" he teased, taking her by the arm and making her slow to his more leisurely step.

"I am, actually. I wasn't lying when I said I was tired. I really need to get home."

Kirk looked at her more carefully. In the subdued lighting in the library he'd only seen how beautiful she was, but here, in the main entrance, he became aware of the shadows under her eyes and the strain around her mouth. It brought his protective instincts to the fore and made his gut clench in concern.

"Is everything okay with you, the baby?" he asked.

He'd been so frustrated by her refusal to consider their marriage that in all honesty he'd been avoiding her these past couple of days. Part of him hoped that absence might make her more willing to reconsider his proposal, while another, less calculating part was learning to deal with not getting his own way. It wasn't something he'd had to do often in adulthood, and he found he didn't like it now any more than he had back when he was a powerless child. But he couldn't force Sally to accede to his suggestion, and she had made it very clear that she wouldn't be coaxed, either. Which was all the more frustrating.

Kirk escorted her down the front stairs of the house and held the door to his car open for her. She stopped in her tracks.

"This isn't your usual SUV, is it?"

"Nope. This one's a hybrid."

She turned and looked at him. "Really?"

"How can I expect everyone else to follow your sustainability proposal if I'm not doing it myself?"

He closed the door as she settled in her seat and resisted the urge to punch the air in triumph—he definitely hadn't missed that look of approval on her face. Score one for him, he thought with a private smile as he walked around the back of the vehicle and to his door. As he got in and secured his seat belt, Sally spoke again.

"And the other managers?"

"As their leases come due on their existing vehicles, even good old Silas will be going hybrid or full electric."

"Seriously?"

"No point in being halfhearted about it, is there?"

"And you approach everything in your life full-out like that?"

He caught her eye and hesitated a few seconds before answering. "When I'm permitted."

She looked away.

"Are you sure you're okay? Not overdoing things?" he asked.

"I'm fine. Did you get my schedule of prenatal visits?"

He nodded. He hated this skirting around the subject he really wanted to discuss, so he took the bull by the horns.

"Sally, I wish you'd change your mind about us marrying. I can promise you my full commitment to making it work. To being a good husband and father."

She shook her head slightly. "I thought we agreed to leave this subject where we finished it."

"Actually, no. *You* said the subject was closed. But *I'm* still very open to negotiation." He started the car and put it in gear, driving smoothly up the driveway and through the automatic gates that swung open as he approached. "I miss what we had."

She stiffened beside him. "What we had was a few brief and highly charged sexual encounters. Nothing more than that."

"Really? Is that how you see it? You know more about my background than any other woman I ever dated."

She snorted. "If they know less than me, then I'm sorry for them. I don't even know what your favorite color is. What kind of food you like. Your favorite drink. Your favorite author. We don't know one another at all."

"Blue, Italian, beer and J. K. Rowling."

"Kirk, it's not enough. And not knowing you isn't the only thing. I don't want to marry you. Please respect that."

Silence fell between them. And then Sally giggled.

"What?" he asked, not feeling at all like laughing given her very solid rejection.

"J. K. Rowling? Really?"

He shrugged. "What's wrong with a little fantasy in a man's life? I've done reality every day for thirty-four years. When I read I like to escape into someone else's world."

Sally fell silent again. When he pulled into the parking area at her apartment, she sighed heavily.

"I apologize for laughing. I didn't mean to poke fun at you—it just seems so incongruous. You strike me as more the type to enjoy self-help books, or male action adventure."

"I read those, too. You asked for my favorite author." He shrugged. "I told you."

He got down from the car and opened her door for her before escorting her up to her apartment. She opened the door and turned to him.

"Thank you for driving me home. I'm sorry if I disappointed you again. Good night."

And before he could reply, she was inside her apartment and the door was firmly closed behind her.

Kirk stood there a full minute before spinning on his heel and heading for the elevator. She might think she'd had the last word on the subject of their marriage, but one thing she hadn't yet learned was that, for him, disappointment only served to whet his determination and appetite for success. One way or another, he'd figure out how to break her walls down. He had to, because somewhere along the line she'd become less of a challenge and more of a necessity in his life.

Fourteen

Sally tried to give Marilyn a breezy smile as she arrived at her father's office. She'd never make it as a spy, she told herself. It was all she could do not to break down and beg Marilyn to explain why she'd done it. It had taken a week, but Kirk's specialists had found a trail, well hidden, of the information Marilyn had misused. She and Marilyn had been called to a meeting with Orson and Kirk to discuss what was going to happen next. Sally knew Kirk wanted to press criminal charges, and he had every right to, but she honestly hoped it wouldn't go that far.

"I don't know what this is about, do you?" Marilyn asked her as she quickly smoothed her always immaculate hair and reapplied her lipstick.

"No," Sally lied, not very convincingly. "Have you heard anything?"

"Not me," Marilyn said with pursed lips and a shake of her head. "But then, since Kirk Tanner has come on the scene, I'm the last to find out about anything, even your pregnancy."

Sally stiffened at the veiled snipe and watched as Marilyn fussed and primped in preparation for the meeting. She wondered again how it had come to this. The woman had been a maternal figure to her for as long as she could remember. It was one thing to betray the company, but the betrayal of Orson and his family went far deeper than that. What on earth had driven her from faithful employee to vindictive one?

Marilyn snapped her compact closed and returned it to her handbag, which she locked in the bottom drawer of her desk.

"Right, we'd better go in, then," she said, standing and squaring her shoulders as if she was preparing to face a firing squad. "Ironic, isn't it? That I was your support person not so long ago and now you're mine?"

Sally could only nod and follow Marilyn into her dad's office. Her eyes went first to Kirk, who wore an expression she'd never seen on his face before and, to be honest, hoped never to see again. Anger simmered behind his startling blue eyes, and his lips were drawn in a thin, straight line of disapproval. Orson, too, looked anything but his usual self. The second she saw him, Marilyn rushed forward.

"Orson, are you all right? You look unwell. Are

you sure you should be here today? I told you you've come back to work too soon."

Orson stepped back from her. "Marilyn, please. Don't fuss—I'm absolutely fine. Take a seat."

"But surely we can put this off until some other time. You probably should be resting."

"Please, sit!" he said bluntly.

Marilyn looked affronted at his tone, her gaze sliding from Orson to Kirk and back again before she sniffed to show her disapproval and finally did as Orson had asked. Sally sat in a chair next to her, perched on the edge of her seat. She knotted her fingers together in her lap and kept her gaze fixed on the floor. Orson resumed his position behind his desk and Kirk drew up another chair next to Marilyn and turned slightly to face her.

Once everyone was settled, Orson began.

"We have had some…difficulties…in the past year with losing business to DuBecTec. At first I thought it was just their good luck, especially with their strengths in networking systems, but as it happened more often, I began to suspect that we had a traitor in our midst here who was feeding information about our prospective clients to our competition."

Sally flicked a look at Marilyn, who shifted in her seat but kept her silence. The tension became so thick you could cut it with a knife.

"And it seems that the traitor was quite happy to set Sally up to take the fall for their insidious and, quite frankly, illegal behavior. I could have forgiven a lot, but I cannot, ever, forgive that."

Sally was shocked to hear the break in her father's voice. She hadn't expected him to bring the suspicions of her own conduct into the equation, but to hear him stand up for her like that came as something of a surprise. He'd barely mentioned the accusations against her when she'd returned to work, but now she could see a cold fury simmering beneath his professional facade. She began to feel some sympathy for Marilyn, but that was soon dashed as the older woman began to speak.

"But Sally was cleared, wasn't she? Of course she was. She had nothing to do with it, I knew that all along and so should you!" Marilyn protested.

"That's right, she had nothing to do with it," Kirk said, rising from his chair and moving to stand beside Orson's desk. "But the strain *you* put her under by planting evidence against her was inexcusable."

"What? Wait. Me?" Marilyn's voice rose in incredulity.

"We have proof, Marilyn. We know who our culprit is," Orson said heavily. "What we don't know is…why?"

"I don't know what you're talking about," Marilyn insisted, but her face had paled and small beads of perspiration had formed on her upper lip. She looked toward Sally. "Tell them, my dear. Tell them I could never be involved in something like that. I love this company and I love your fa—"

Her voice cut off before she finished her sentence,

as if she'd suddenly realized she'd revealed too much. She slumped back in her chair, her gaze shifting from Orson to Kirk and then Sally before settling back on Orson.

"I have loved you for thirty years, Orson Harrison. And this is how you treat me?"

Orson, too, had paled. "This is about your behavior—not mine," he said gruffly. "And you know there has only ever been one woman for me."

Marilyn laughed, a brittle, bitter sound. "Well, I was good enough for you once, wasn't I?"

"I told you then and I'll tell you now, it was a wretched mistake. I was a grieving man reaching out for comfort, and I never should have put you in that position."

Sally looked at her father in shock. He'd had an affair with Marilyn after her mother's death? How on earth had they continued to work together for so long after that? Had Marilyn's unrequited love been what kept her, day in and day out, at her desk in the hope that one day Orson Harrison would change his mind? Sally swallowed against the lump that had solidified in her throat.

All her life Marilyn had been there. With no mother to turn to, Marilyn had been the one to explain about the things girls needed to know about their bodies, to talk about what was right and wrong when it came to boys, to take her shopping for her first bra. To dry her tears when her best friend from elementary school moved away or when a high school crush broke her heart.

At every major turning point in her life, Marilyn had been the female perspective she'd needed. Now she was learning that Marilyn had loved Orson for all those years. And yet, despite all of that, despite all those years, she'd been quite happy to let Sally take blame for something she herself had done—even knowing how much that stigma would hurt Sally and Orson.

"I can't believe you were going to let me take the fall for this, Marilyn."

"Oh, please. As if it would have been an issue for you. Your father would never press charges against you. And besides, it's not as if you need the work. You were born with a silver spoon in your mouth. No, it would all have been neatly swept under the carpet and maybe, just maybe, the shock would have been enough for Orson to finally see *me* again. Do you know why he never took our affair any further? Because of you. Because he didn't want you to feel he was replacing your mother. After you freaked out at the funeral, he realized how weak you were. How needy you'd become. So he put me on the back burner."

Orson rose to his feet. "That's not true!"

Marilyn also stood. "Isn't it? It certainly felt like that to me. Do you realize what I've given up for you? Everything, that's what. My youth. My hopes. My dreams for a family of my own. But you didn't care. And when I thought you might finally be coming around, that with the right encouragement you might step away from the business and maybe actually look at retirement with me still there by your side, what do you do? You merge with *him*! The son of the man who almost destroyed this company just as it was getting off the ground!"

She pointed a finger sharply in the air in Kirk's direction. "Even after your heart attack you kept working, when a rational man would have given up. Don't you see? I did all that for you, for us! Can't you understand what it was like for me? How I was looking down the barrel of retirement alone? I gave my life for you, Orson. And in return you gave me nothing."

Kirk stepped forward. "I think you've said enough, Marilyn. You are hereby relieved of your duties at Harrison Tanner Tech. I'm calling security to come and hold you until the police can be called so we can press charges."

"No, wait," Orson said, looking a lot older than he had only short moments ago. "This is my fault."

"Dad, no. It's not," Sally cried, pushing upright out of her chair.

"Honey, I'm man enough to admit my mistakes. I shouldn't have turned to Marilyn for comfort, but I made a much bigger error when I expected there not to be any repercussions. Marilyn, I'm sorry. I should have taken better care of you at the time. I should have found you employment elsewhere instead of continuing to take your loyalty to me for granted."

"Orson, she betrayed everyone here with her actions. She could have destroyed everything," Kirk argued, his hands clenched futilely at his sides.

"But we stopped her in time, didn't we? I don't

want to press charges." Marilyn gasped in shock, and Orson fixed his gaze on her. "Even though they are warranted. What you did threatened not only my family but the families of all the staff here. It was unforgivable."

"I did it for you," Marilyn repeated brokenly.

"No." He shook his head sadly. "You did it for you. But I will right my wrong." He mentioned a sum of money that made even Sally's eyebrows rise a little. "I will offer you that severance on the condition that you leave Washington, never come back and never contact me again. The legal department will draw up a nondisclosure agreement. Upon signing, you will agree to say absolutely nothing about what transpired during any of your time working here. You will never share information about the company, me or my family ever again. Do you understand me?"

Marilyn sank back in her chair and nodded weakly. "You're sending me away?"

"I'm giving you a chance to make a new life, Marilyn. The choice is yours. Take it and rebuild, or stay and face the consequences of what you've done."

Not surprisingly, Marilyn accepted his offer with the scrap of dignity she had left. As she turned to leave the room, she looked at Sally.

"You think it's all about work and making a name for yourself here, but it's not. One day you'll be just like me. Alone."

Sally stood to face her. "No, I won't be like you, Marilyn, because I could never do what you've done to hurt the people who've always supported you."

* * *

Kirk escorted Marilyn from the office and requested security to accompany her from the building once she'd removed her personal effects. Anger still roiled through him, unresolved. He didn't agree with Orson's offer, didn't trust Marilyn as far as he could kick her, but he had to abide by the older man's dictates.

Marilyn looked broken as she moved about the outer office, packing her personal mementos. All the fight and fire gone, every one of her years etched deeply into the lines on her face.

So much damage, so much risk—and all for unrequited love? It wasn't as if she'd even done it out of spite or greed. She'd done it to try to force the man she loved to notice her—to stop being the work-driven tycoon he'd always been.

And wasn't he just like that, too? Hadn't he modeled himself on Orson Harrison his whole adult life? Didn't he aspire to enjoy the same success Orson had? But at what cost? After Marilyn had been escorted away, Kirk sighed heavily and returned to Orson's office, his thoughts still whirling. He'd asked Sally to marry him, more than once, without stopping to consider what he was offering her. Oh, sure, he said he wanted to be a hands-on parent—there for his child every step of the way. But had he even once stopped to consider Sally's feelings?

What about *her* needs, her dreams for the future? Had he ever asked her about what she wanted? No, it had all been about him. Him and his desire to be everything his father wasn't. The realization was an unpleasant one.

He'd never considered himself a selfish man—he'd always bestowed that honor on his father, who always put his needs and addictions first. But looking at himself right now, Kirk found his actions wanting. He needed to change. He needed to be a man worthy of a woman like Sally Harrison if he was ever going to win her.

Kirk closed Orson's office door behind him and sat heavily in the chair Marilyn had vacated.

"She's gone?" Orson asked.

He still looked drawn, but beneath his pallor Kirk detected the steely determination that had made Orson the successful man he was. On the other side of the desk, Sally looked shaken, as well, but he saw the same strength in her. He wondered if either father or daughter realized how alike they truly were.

"Yes," Kirk answered. "The legal department is standing by for your instructions."

"Good, good. I'll get to that next. Have you two got a few minutes? We need to talk."

"I'm okay for a while," Sally said. "But if you'd rather, Dad, we can do this later. I know you're upset. I'm pretty stunned myself. I trusted her all my life."

"And I trusted her with mine. It's taught me a painful but valuable lesson. My own lapse in judgment in having that brief affair with Marilyn led her to nurse false hopes that there could one day be more between us. For myself, all I ever felt after that encounter was guilt and disappointment in myself. I guess that's one of the reasons I kept her on here. I felt I needed to make it up to her that I couldn't offer her more." He sighed and shifted a set of papers on the desk in front of him.

"Looking back won't change anything, but we can look forward, and my heart attack was a long overdue wake-up call. I've been reevaluating things, and I believe I am ready to step back and relinquish many of my responsibilities here. I want to be able to enjoy the rest of my life, enjoy my grandchild when he or she comes along. I want to take time to focus on what really matters before it's all taken from me."

"Dad, are you sure? Medically there's no reason—"

"No, medically there is no reason for me not to stay in this saddle for a good many more years yet. The thing is, I don't want to anymore. And I'm starting to think I don't need to. The company will be in fine hands even if I step back, and you... I suppose part of the reason I stayed was because I felt the need to look out for you. I turned to Marilyn for advice about you once your mother passed away, especially when it became apparent that you were struggling with your phobia. When Marilyn told me not to push you, I didn't. In fact, I didn't ever encourage you to reach your full potential, did I? I could have done a better job in teaching you to reach past your fears, but I deferred to what I believed was her better judgment instead of listening to my own heart as your father. And despite all that, you strove for excellence anyway. Look at you now—head of your own department here and motivating the entire firm to embrace sustainability. You've achieved that by your own hard work, not from any handout from me.

"I know it hasn't been easy for you here. I've heard the rumors that you only got your position because you're my daughter. Despite—or maybe because of—my doing my best to protect you, there are others who've made things difficult for you. And still, you've never quit, never given up."

"I get that from you, Dad. When it comes to tenacity, you're king, right?" Sally smiled, and Kirk felt his gut twist at the bittersweet expression on her face.

Sally's father's words echoed in his head. He'd been just the same, just as determined to try to shelter and protect Sally—to make her decisions for her rather than trust her to make her own. To be her own person.

"I'm very proud of you, Sally, I want you to know that. I'm not just proud of you, the woman, I'm incredibly proud of what you have achieved here. If you were anyone else, I would have been fast-tracking you on a development program—pushing you up through the ranks to senior management. But I obviously had my own prejudices when it came to my daughter in the workplace. So, I want to ask you a question. Do you want to take on the additional training and responsibilities that come with escalating your seniority in the company?"

"It's what I've always wanted," Sally said in a strong voice.

Her blue eyes glowed with excitement, and Kirk

began to see the woman she truly was. Not just the beautiful blonde who'd turned his head in a bar one night. Not just the lover who'd tipped his world upside down. And not the woman who now carried his child. Instead he saw who she should have been all along. A strong, intelligent individual who deserved to shine.

"But what about my phobia?" she asked. "Won't that be a problem?"

"We will find a way to work around it. You're getting better—I'm told your sustainability presentation was going very well until you fainted." Orson's tone was teasing and indulgent. "Right, that's decided then. Kirk, she's going to need support from you in this. Can I rely on you to be there for her?"

"If it's what Sally wants, then I will be there for her every way she needs me," Kirk said in a steady voice.

"Good," Orson replied. "Now, if you'd give Sally and me a moment or two alone? Then perhaps you and I can meet over lunch to iron out a few changes."

"Sure." Kirk got up to leave and paused at Sally's side. He resisted the urge to lay a hand on her shoulder. It wasn't what he'd do with any other colleague, and his desire to touch her would have to be firmly kept in rein from now on. "I'll call you this afternoon to schedule some time to discuss your plan going forward, okay?"

"Thank you," she said with an inclination of her head. "I'll look forward to it."

And yet, as Kirk left the office, he had the distinct impression she looked forward to anything but.

He'd created that resistance between them with his behavior from the very first moment he'd met her. He had a lot of work to do if he hoped to build their relationship to any kind of level where she would let him back in again.

Fifteen

Sally watched her father reorder the papers on his desk again. Clearly, he was uncomfortable with what he was about to say to her. Never hugely demonstrative, to hear him offer the words of pride he'd given her today had been a golden moment for her. For the first time since that awful moment at her mother's funeral when she'd frozen in front of all the mourners, she felt as though she had his attention for all the right reasons.

Orson cleared his throat. "Sally, are you sure you want to follow this leadership track?"

"As I said, Dad, it's what I've always wanted. I just never thought you believed in me enough to suggest it, to be honest."

Sally cringed inwardly at her words. She'd never

had this kind of discussion with her father before, but obviously the time for openness between them was long overdue. They'd each always done what was expected of them, without a thought for what either of them really wanted. Orson was right—it was time for change.

"Hmm." Her father nodded, then looked up and pinned her with a look. "What are you going to do about your feelings for Kirk?"

"My what?"

"Don't play coy with me, my girl. It's no use denying it. I might not have been the best father in the world, but I know my daughter. You love him, don't you?"

Sally sat frozen in her chair. She'd pigeonholed her feelings for Kirk as inconvenient at best, especially when it was clear he didn't love her. But had her developing love for Kirk been so painfully obvious? Her father continued.

"I guess what I really want to know is, are you going to act on those feelings, or are you going to let the opportunity for a long and happy married life slide by you because you're too afraid to speak up for what you really want?"

"I'm not afraid. I know what I want, and it begins and ends with this company," she said bravely.

"Are you sure about that? Your mother and I didn't have long enough together. There isn't a day that goes by that I don't think of her and miss her with an ache that never fades. Work gives me something to do—but it's no substitute for her. Don't be like me, honey. Please. You and my grandbaby deserve more than that."

Sally looked at her father in surprise. Were those tears shimmering in his eyes? Surely not. But then, he'd changed since his heart attack. He'd obviously spent time reevaluating his life and found it wanting. He was right, though. She had to give her own and the baby's future careful thought. Obviously she wouldn't block Kirk's access to his child, but marriage? She still wanted to hold out for what she believed marriage to be—a deep commitment to blend the lives of two people who would love each other until their dying breath, and beyond.

She chose her words very carefully. "I have given it a lot of thought, and I reached my decision. I would ask that you respect my choice. I want more than just a marriage and security. Between the trust fund Mom left me and my salary, I'm in the fortunate enough position that I certainly don't need a partner for financial security—even with the baby. But if I'm to consider marrying anyone, I need to be certain that they can provide what I need on an emotional level, and right now I don't think he can."

Orson slumped in his chair, disappointment and acceptance chasing across his features.

"Thank you for being honest with me about how you feel, Dad," Sally continued. "It means more to me than you probably realize to know you care. And I'm sorry it isn't what you wanted to hear, but this is my life and I have to take care of me, too, not just the baby."

She rose and went around to him and wrapped her arms about his shoulders. "I love you, Dad."

"I love you, too, honey."

Sally went back downstairs to her department and shut herself in her office, but she couldn't concentrate on the work in front of her. Her mind was whirling with everything that had happened today. So much to take in. But if her father and Marilyn's example had taught her anything, it was that she shouldn't settle for a relationship that was anything less than what she truly wanted.

She wanted more than just to settle for the sensible option. More for her baby, more for herself. And one day maybe she could have that. Working her way up the ladder, taking more responsibility here at work was all she'd ever wanted careerwise, and now, finally, she was on track to attain that. If she found a truly fulfilling love, then she'd embrace it. If not, she'd be fine without it. She didn't doubt for a minute that she'd be able to balance motherhood and work. Of course it wouldn't be easy, but women around the world combined successful, high-octane careers with parenting. She would make adjustments and she'd cope.

And, with that, Sally was finally completely satisfied with her decision. She would not compromise. She would not marry without a reciprocated love. Despite their chemistry, she and Kirk both deserved more out of a relationship than that. They would successfully coparent, the way countless others had before them. And even if seeing him every day—being mentored by him—would likely be absolute physical and emotional torture, she would do it rather than compromise on her values.

You couldn't make someone love you—Marilyn was proof of that. All the wishing, hoping or pushing couldn't do it. And living with unrequited love was equivalent to a lifelong sentence of unhappiness.

If she was certain of anything, it was that she deserved so much more than that.

Kirk kept his distance from Sally even though it killed him. Orson had cut his hours back to two and a half days a week, which put a great deal more responsibility on Kirk's plate. Thankfully, he'd been able to hire a new PA, and the woman was a marvel at organization. She also had the uncanny ability to anticipate his needs, which made his life roll a great deal more smoothly.

Without being obvious, Kirk kept a close eye on Sally. She'd quickly settled into a pattern, attending the leadership program mentoring sessions with regularity. Judging by the standard of work she was returning to him, she was spending a lot of hours outside the office on the tasks assigned to her. He was surprised at her tenacity, but then again, didn't her résumé reflect that she'd been tenacious all her life?

She was doing excellent work with the sustainability rollout. It was also being implemented in the other branches of HTT, which meant some travel time for her, both by air and road. He'd heard she was slowly overcoming her speaking issues, too. Granted, the groups she was dealing with were all smaller than here at the head office, but Nick had reported back regularly that she was doing better with each presentation.

He hated it when she was away and had recruited Nick to ensure that she ate regularly and well. The other man had been surprised but had taken it in stride. It meant that when Kirk made his nightly calls to her while Sally traveled, he didn't have to come across like a drill sergeant checking she was taking her vitamins and supplements and getting enough sleep.

Christmas had come and gone. Sally was sixteen weeks pregnant now and had the cutest baby bump. Kirk had bookmarked a website on his laptop that showed him the stages of pregnancy, and he marveled every day at the changes that were happening in Sally's body. The realization that it was his child growing inside her still took his breath away. Their latest prenatal appointment, where they'd heard the baby's heartbeat, had made the pregnancy overwhelmingly and incredibly real and had left him feeling oddly emotional.

He looked at his watch. She should be back home from her New York presentation by now. Her flight had been due in about ninety minutes ago. Would she object to him making a check-in call? Too bad if she did. Suddenly he had the overwhelming urge to hear her voice.

Except when he dialed her apartment, there was no reply. That was odd. He called her cell phone and got an automated message saying her phone was off or out of range. A sick feeling crept through him. He wasn't one to jump to conclusions, but something didn't feel right.

Kirk was just about to call Nick's cell phone when his screen lit up with an incoming call. It was Orson.

"Kirk, it's Sally. She's been taken to the hospital."

A shaft of dread sliced through him, stealing his breath and making his heart hammer in his chest.

"What is it, what's wrong? Is it the baby?"

"I'm not sure, and she's not answering her phone. I just got out of a meeting to find that she'd left me a message saying she'd landed but that her leg was sore and swollen and that Benton was taking her to the hospital to be checked out. A swollen leg after flying, that's not good, is it?"

It wasn't good, not under any circumstances. Along with learning about the growth of the baby, Kirk had been driving himself crazy reading about risks in pregnancy, and he knew that a swollen leg could be indicative of a blood clot.

"Where do they have her?"

"She didn't say. She told me not to worry, but it's kind of difficult not to when you love someone, right?"

Orson's question reverberated through Kirk's mind. Was that what this sudden abject fear was? Love?

"Leave it with me, Orson. I'll see what I can find out and let you know the minute I hear anything."

"Good, thanks. And if she calls me, I'll be sure to tell you."

Kirk called Nick's phone and finally got hold of him, except the man could offer him no help. Sally had apparently been fine when he'd left her at the airport with Benton. Kirk hung up as quickly as he could and called the bodyguard, who was in the ER waiting room at the hospital. The moment Kirk had the details and had shared them with Orson, he was in his car and on his way to the hospital.

He released Benton to go home as soon as he arrived, promising to let the man know Sally's prognosis the moment he heard anything. Then began the struggle to get some information on Sally's condition. But it appeared that no amount of coercion, charm or outright badgering would budge the staff. And so began the longest two hours of his life.

This was far worse than when his mother had died. By the time her cancer had been diagnosed, it had been too late for treatment and they'd had a few months to come to terms with things—as much as anyone came to terms with impending death. But he'd known and understood every step of her journey. Had made it his business to. This, though—it was out of his control, and he found he didn't like it one bit.

Fear for the baby was one thing, but a possible blood clot was a serious business and could potentially put Sally's life at risk. The very idea of losing her terrified him. He'd agreed to abide by her wish not to marry, as much as he'd hated it, but right now he wished he had pushed her harder to accept him. Then he'd have the right to know what was happening, how she was.

He got up and began to pace, but the ER was a busy place and there was hardly enough room for anything, so he found a spot against the wall and stared at the double doors leading to the treatment area and waited. And, as the hands on the clock on the wall ticked interminably by, he couldn't help remembering what Orson had said. *She told me not to worry, but it's kind of difficult not to when you love someone, right?*

Love. He'd never imagined he'd ever know what true, romantic love was. He'd seen what love had done for his mother and how her affection for his father had slowly been crushed out of her until all that was left was sadness and despair. When he'd created his life plan, he'd known he was prepared to settle for respect and affection in marriage without the soaring highs or devastating lows that so many people experienced on the road to happily-ever-after. He didn't have time for that, didn't need it, didn't want it.

And yet, he wanted Sally. Wanted everything to do with her—to be by her side, to guide her and see her reach her career goals, to watch her become a mother and to traverse the minefields of parenthood together. But most of all, he finally realized, he wanted to love her. He wanted the right to be the one she turned to in times of trouble or in times of joy. He wanted to be the one to fill her heart with happiness, to take her problems and make them go away. He wanted to laugh with her, live with her and love her forever.

Kirk realized he was shaking. The yearning inside him had grown so strong, so overwhelming that tears now pricked at the back of his eyes. He hadn't cried since his mother passed, and then only in the privacy of his own home. But this—it was raw, it was real and he'd never felt so damned helpless in his entire life.

A movement behind the doors caught his attention and he saw Sally being wheeled out by an orderly— a fistful of papers in her hand and a tired smile on her face. A smile that faded away in surprise when she saw him striding toward her.

"Kirk? What are you doing here?"

"I'm here for *you*, Sally," he said, and he'd never meant anything more seriously in his life.

Unfortunately the ER waiting room was not the place for the discussion they desperately needed to have.

She looked a little disconcerted but then nodded. "I'm fine—honestly. I've been cleared to go home."

"Everything's okay?"

"Yes. It was just an overreaction on Benton's part. I mentioned my leg was a bit achy and swollen when he met me at SeaTac, and he insisted on bringing me straight here."

"I'm giving him a bonus. That's exactly what he should have done. You didn't give him grief about that, did you?" he asked as they walked toward the exit.

"I was going to, but then I thought about the traveling I've been doing lately and, to be totally honest,

I got scared about what it could have been and was only too happy for someone else to make the decisions for me. But why are you here?"

"Orson called me. He got your message, which was pretty scant on details and left us both worried."

"I should call him," she answered, reaching in her bag for her phone, which she turned on. "Oh, I've got missed calls. Dad—" she scrolled through the list "—and you."

"We were concerned."

Those three words didn't even go halfway to explaining how worried he'd been. They reached the parking area and Kirk helped her into the car and waited, not bothering to start the car yet, as she called her dad to reassure him that everything was okay.

"No, no, I'm fine. I don't need to come to your place. Everything checked out normal—just a bit of fluid retention. No, Dad, it's really nothing to worry about. They did scans and everything."

Eventually she hung up and sighed heavily.

"Tired?" Kirk asked.

"Worn-out."

"Let me take you home. You're sure you don't want to go to your father's? Or my place?"

"What part of 'I'm fine' don't you men seem to understand? Look—" she yanked her discharge papers from her bag and shook them at him "—everything is normal."

But there was a wobble to her voice that struck Kirk straight to his heart. She'd been afraid and alone. He didn't stop to think twice. He simply reached out his arms and closed them around her, pulling her toward him. In the confines of the car it was a challenge to offer her the comfort he knew she needed, but he did his best.

At first she stiffened and began to pull away, but then she sagged into him and he felt her arms reach around his waist.

"I'm so glad you're okay, Sally. Quite frankly, I was terrified for you. I never want to feel that afraid again."

She sniffed, and he loosened his hold so he could grab a bunch of tissues from the glove box. She took them from him and wiped her eyes and blew her nose.

"Thanks. Can we go home now?"

"Sure."

He waited for her to buckle her seat belt before doing the same, and then he drove to her apartment. Once there, he followed her inside.

"Sit down," he instructed. "I'll make you a hot drink."

It was a measure of how tired she was that she didn't protest, just merely offered her thanks. Kirk quickly brewed a cup of chamomile tea and brought it to her. The china cup and saucer felt incongruously delicate in his large hand, a simile for the delicacy of their relationship and how he could all too easily damage it if he didn't use care, he realized.

He sat down with her as she sipped her tea, and when she was finished he put an arm around her, encouraging her to snuggle against him and relax.

She felt so right in his arms. Sexual attraction aside, there was something incredibly satisfying about just being with her. And that was a crucial part of getting to know one another that they'd skipped. Maybe if he'd been more restrained, had shown more of his interest in getting to know all of her and not just her body, they'd have stood a better chance.

But now he had something to fight for. He knew, without any doubt, that he'd fallen crazy in love with this incredible, strong woman. He just hadn't let himself see that his feelings went deeper than physical appeal. Hadn't wanted the mess and the clutter in his emotional life that he knew being in love could bring. Today had taught him that he'd been so very wrong.

"Sally?" he asked, wondering if she'd fallen asleep.

"Hmm?" she answered.

"Could I stay tonight?"

She shuffled away from him, and he felt the loss as if a piece of him had been sliced away.

"Stay? Here?"

"I can sleep on the couch. I don't expect… I just need to know you're going to be okay and to be on hand to get you anything you need."

When she started to protest, he put up a hand.

"Seriously, I know you're worn-out with the visit to New York and flying home and having been to the hospital. And if I left you here alone, I wouldn't sleep a wink—I'd be up all night, worrying about you. Let me help you, for both our sakes, okay?"

She stared at him, her blue eyes underlined by

shadows of weariness that made him want to do nothing more than swoop her up into his arms and take her to her bed and insist she stay there for the next week. But he didn't even have the right to suggest it.

"Okay, if that's what you want."

"Thank you."

"But why, Kirk? You know I'm okay, don't you? I don't need to be monitored or anything."

"I know. *I* just need to be sure. Today scared me more than I thought it was possible to be. It brought a few truths home to roost."

Sally raised her brows. "Oh?"

"It made me take a good long hard look at myself. At what I want. I meant what I said at the hospital. I'm here for you. And I really wish I had the right to be here for you on a permanent basis."

She sighed and looked away. "Kirk, we've discussed this. I told you I don't want to marry you."

"I know. I've been an idiot. You were right to turn down what I was offering. I thought that all it would take was for us to agree to be a couple, but today taught me that there's so much more than that. Yes, I wanted the dream—the beautiful wife, the perfect child, the career every man envies. But I wasn't prepared to work hard enough for any of that. I wasn't prepared to make myself vulnerable or even admit that I needed anyone else to achieve my goals. To be totally honest, I was prepared to accept something that would look more like a business partnership than a marriage, and it absolutely shames me to admit it."

Sally frowned, looking uncertain. "What are you saying?"

"I'm saying that I didn't believe you needed love, real love, to make a successful marriage. But now I know that for a marriage to really mean something, the people have to truly mean something to each other."

She nodded slowly. "That's my understanding of it, too. I won't settle for less."

"Me either. Standing there in that ER waiting room, knowing I had no right to be there with you, no right to support you the way you deserve to be supported—" His voice cracked, and he rubbed a hand across his face. "Sally, it was the toughest thing I've ever done in my life, and it made me realize something very important."

"And that is?"

"That I love you. I'm not a man who is big on expressing my feelings, but please believe me when I say that today was hell on earth for me. You mean more to me than any person I've ever known. I want to spend the rest of my life proving that to you, if you'll let me."

"And the baby?"

"And the baby, too, of course. But no matter what, I love you—and whether you agree to marry me or not, I always will."

Sally's eyes washed with tears and she looked away. For a moment he thought she was going to turn him down, but then she looked back at him and a tentative smile began to pull at her lips.

"Always?" she asked, her smile broadening.

"Forever. I mean it."

"And I'll continue in the leadership program at work?"

"Of course. You're a valuable member of the team, why wouldn't I want you there?"

"Forever, you say?"

He nodded, holding his breath.

"I couldn't accept your proposal without love, Kirk. My parents had a short but loving marriage. No one deserves less than that. Even you."

He looked at her in confusion. Was she turning him down again? Was she saying she couldn't love him? It would kill a piece of him to accept her decision, but he'd do it if that was what made her happy.

Sally reached out and took his hands in hers. "Thank you for opening up your heart to me tonight. I needed to hear it—needed to know that you had it in you to feel as deeply for me as I feel for you, because I love you, too."

Kirk sucked air into his lungs, barely able to believe the words she'd just said.

"Thank you," he said on a whoosh of air. "You have no idea how happy that makes me."

She nodded and leaned in until her lips were just a whisper away from his. "Me too," she answered before kissing him. She drew away far too quickly and smiled. "There's just one thing I need to ask of you."

"Anything," he hastened to say. "Name it and I'll move heaven and earth to make sure it's yours."

She shrugged and gave him another of those beautiful sweet smiles. "You probably don't have to go that far," she teased.

"What do you want from me?" he asked.

"Will you marry me?"

"I absolutely will," he said and bent to kiss her again.

When they drew apart, Kirk looked at Sally, stunned by the gift she'd bestowed on him. "You won't regret it. I promise to spend the rest of my life making sure you don't."

"As I will, too," she answered solemnly.

For a moment they simply sat there and drank in each other's presence, but then Kirk looked around them. "So, about me sleeping on the couch..."

Sally laughed out loud, a full-throttle belly laugh that immediately had Kirk responding in kind.

"I think we can forget the couch tonight, don't you?" she said, getting to her feet and offering him her hand.

And, as Kirk walked with Sally into her bedroom, he knew that he was the luckiest man on earth. Lucky to have learned the truth about love before it was too late. Lucky to have a child on the way. And most of all, lucky to have this woman in his life.

* * * * *

If you enjoyed this book, you'll love
CAN'T HARDLY BREATHE,
the next book in New York Times
bestselling author Gena Showalter's
ORIGINAL HEARTBREAKERS *series.*
Read on for a sneak peek!

DANIEL PORTER SAT at the edge of the bed. Again and again he dismantled and rebuilt his Glock 17. Before he removed the magazine, he racked the slide to ensure no ammunition remained in the chamber. He lifted the upper portion of the semiautomatic, detached the recoil spring as well as the barrel. Then he put everything back together.

Rinse and repeat.

Some things you had to do over and over, until every cell in your body learned to perform the task on autopilot. That way, when bullets started flying, you'd react the right way—immediately—without having to check a training manual.

When his eyelids grew heavy, he placed the gun on the nightstand and stretched out across the mattress only to toss and turn. Staying at the Strawberry Inn without a woman wasn't one of his brightest ideas. Sex kept him distracted from the many horrors that lived inside his mind. After multiple overseas military tours, constant gunfights, car bombs, finding one friend after another blown to pieces, watching his targets collapse because he'd gotten a green light and pulled the trigger…his sanity had long since packed up and moved out.

Daniel scrubbed a clammy hand over his face. In the quiet of the room, he began to notice the mental chorus in the back of his mind. Muffled screams he'd heard since his first tour of duty. He pulled at hanks of his hair, but the screams only escalated.

This. This was the reason he refused to commit to a woman. Well, one of many reasons. He was too messed up, his past too violent, his present too uncertain.

A man who looked at a TV remote as if it were a bomb about to detonate had no business inviting an innocent civilian into his crazy.

He'd even forgotten how to laugh.

No, not true. Since his return to Strawberry Valley, two people had defied the odds and amused him. His best friend slash spirit animal Jessie Kay West… and Dottie.

My name is Dorothea.

She'd been two grades behind him, had always kept to herself, had never caused any trouble and had never attended any parties. A "goody-goody," many had called her. Daniel remembered feeling sorry for her, a sweetheart targeted by the town bully.

Today, his reaction to her endearing shyness and unintentional insults had shocked him. Somehow she'd turned him on so fiercely, he'd felt as if *years* had passed since he'd last had sex rather than a few hours. But then, everything about his most recent encounter with Dot—Dorothea had shocked him.

Upon returning from his morning run, he'd stood in the doorway of his room, watching her work. As she'd vacuumed, she'd wiggled her hips, dancing to music with a different beat than the song playing on his iPod.

Control had been beyond him—he'd hardened instantly.

He'd noticed her appeal on several other occasions, of course. How could he not? Her eyes, once too big for her face, were now a perfect fit and the most amazing shade of green. Like shamrocks or lucky charms, framed by the thickest, blackest lashes he'd ever seen. Those eyes were an absolute showstopper. Her lips were plump and heart-shaped, a fantasy made flesh. And her body...

Daniel grinned up at the ceiling. He suspected she had serious curves underneath her scrubs. The way the material had tightened over her chest when she'd moved...the lushness of her ass when she'd bent over...every time he'd looked at her, he'd sworn he'd developed early-onset arrhythmia.

With her eyes, lips and corkscrew curls, she reminded him of a living doll. *Blow her up, and she'll blow me.* He really wanted to play with her.

But he wouldn't. Ever. She lived right here in town.

When Daniel first struck up a friendship with Jessie Kay, his father expressed hope for a Christmas wedding and grandkids soon after. The moment Daniel had broken the news—no wedding, no kids—Virgil teared up.

Lesson learned. When it came to Strawberry Valley girls, Virgil would always think long-term, and he would always be disappointed when the relationship ended. Stress wasn't good for his ticker. Daniel loved the old grump with every fiber of his being, wanted him around as long as possible.

Came back to care for him. Not going to make things worse.

Bang, bang, bang!

Daniel palmed his semiautomatic and plunged to the floor to use the bed as a shield. As a bead of sweat rolled into his eye, his finger twitched on the trigger. The screams in his head were drowned out by the sound of his thundering heartbeat.

Bang, bang!

He muttered a curse. The door. Someone was knocking on the door.

Disgusted with himself, he glanced at the clock on the nightstand—1:08 a.m.

As he stood, his dog tags clinked against his mother's locket, the one he'd worn since her death. He pulled on the wrinkled, ripped jeans he'd tossed earlier and anchored his gun against his lower back.

Forgoing the peephole, he looked through the crack in the window curtains. His gaze landed on a dark, wild mass of corkscrew curls, and his frown deepened. Only one woman in town had hair like that, every strand made for tangling in a man's fists.

Concern overshadowed a fresh surge of desire

as he threw open the door. Hinges squeaked, and Dorothea paled. But a fragrant cloud of lavender enveloped him, and his head fogged; desire suddenly overshadowed concern.

Down, boy.

She met his gaze for a split second, then ducked her head and wrung her hands. Before, freckles had covered her face. Now a thick layer of makeup hid them. Unfortunate. He liked those freckles, often imagined—

Nothing.

"Is something wrong?" On alert, he scanned left…right… The hallway was empty, no signs of danger.

As many times as he'd stayed at the inn, Dorothea had only ever spoken to him while cleaning his room. Which had always prompted his early-morning departures. There'd been no reason to grapple with temptation.

"I'm fine," she said, and gulped. Her shallow inhalations came a little too quickly, and her cheeks grew chalk white. "Super fine."

How was her tone shrill and breathy at the same time?

He relaxed his battle stance, though his confusion remained. "Why are you here?"

"I…uh… Do you need more towels?"

"Towels?" His gaze roamed over the rest of her, as if drawn by an invisible force—disappointment struck. She wore a bulky, ankle-length raincoat, hiding the body underneath. Had a storm rolled in? He listened but heard no claps of thunder. "No, thank you. I'm good."

"Okay." She licked her porn-star lips and toyed with the tie around her waist. "Yes, I'll have coffee with you."

Coffee? "Now?"

A defiant nod, those corkscrew curls bouncing.

He barked out a laugh, surprised, amazed and delighted by her all over again. "What's really going on, Dorothea?"

Her eyes widened. "My name. You remembered this time." When he stared at her, expectant, she cleared her throat. "Right. The reason I'm here. I just… I wanted to talk to you." The color returned to her cheeks, a sexy blush spilling over her skin. "May I come in? Please. Before someone sees me."

Mistake. That blush gave a man ideas.

Besides, what could Miss Mathis have to say to him? He ran through a mental checklist of possible problems. His bill—nope, already paid in full. His father's health—nope, Daniel would have been called directly.

If he wanted answers, he'd have to deal with Dorothea…alone…with a bed nearby…

Swallowing a curse, he stepped aside.

She rushed past him as if her feet were on fire, the scent of lavender strengthening. His mouth watered.

I could eat her up.

But he wouldn't. Wouldn't even take a nibble.

"Shut the door. Please," she said, a tremor in her voice.

He hesitated but ultimately obeyed. "Would you like a beer while the coffee brews?"

"Yes, please." She spotted the six-pack he'd brought with him, claimed one of the bottles and popped the cap.

He watched with fascination as she drained the contents.

She wiped her mouth with the back of her wrist and belched softly into her fist. "Thanks. I needed that."

He tried not to smile as he grabbed the pot. "Let's get you that coffee."

"No worries. I'm not thirsty." She placed the empty bottle on the dresser. Her gaze darted around the room, a little wild, a lot nervous. She began to pace in front of him. She wasn't wearing shoes, revealing toenails painted yellow and orange, like her fingernails.

More curious by the second, he eased onto the edge of the bed. "Tell me what's going on."

"All right." Her tongue slipped over her lips, moistening both the upper and lower, and the fly of his jeans tightened. In an effort to keep his hands to himself, he fisted the comforter. "I can't really tell you. I have to show you."

"Show me, then." *And leave.* She had to leave. Soon.

"Yes," she croaked. Her trembling worsened as she untied the raincoat...

The material fell to the floor.

Daniel's heart stopped beating. His brain short-circuited. Dorothea Mathis was gloriously, wonderfully naked; she had more curves than he'd suspected, generous curves, *gorgeous* curves.

Was he drooling? He might be drooling.

She wasn't a living doll, he decided, but a 1950s pinup. *Lord save me.* She had the kind of body other women abhorred but men adored. *He* adored. A vine with thorns and holly was etched around the outside of one breast, ending in a pink bloom just over her heart.

Sweet Dorothea Mathis had a tattoo. He wanted to touch. He *needed* to touch.

A moment of rational thought intruded. Strawberry Valley girls were off-limits…his dad…disappointment… But…

Dorothea's soft, lush curves *deserved* to be touched. Though makeup still hid the freckles on her face, the sweet little dots covered the rest of her alabaster skin. A treasure map for his tongue.

I'll start up top and work my way down. Slowly.

She had a handful of scars on her abdomen and thighs, beautiful badges of strength and survival. More paths for his tongue to follow.

As he studied her, drinking her in, one of her arms draped over her breasts, shielding them from his view. With her free hand, she covered the apex of her thighs, and no shit, he almost whimpered. Such bounty should *never* be covered.

"I want…to sleep with you," she stammered. "One time. Only one time. Afterward, I don't want to speak with you about it. Or about anything. We'll avoid each other for the rest of our lives."

One night of no-strings sex? Yes, please. He wanted her. Here. Now.

For hours and hours…

No. No, no, no. If he slept with the only maid at the only inn in town, he'd have to stay in the city with all future dates, over an hour away from his dad. What if Virgil had another heart attack?

Daniel leaped off the bed to swipe up the rain-coat. A darker blush stained Dorothea's cheeks…and spread…and though he wanted to watch the color deepen, he fit the material around her shoulders.

"You…you don't want me." Horror contorted her features as she spun and raced to the door.

His reflexes were well honed; they had to be. They were the only reason he hadn't come home from his tours of duty in a box. Before she could exit, he raced behind her and flattened his hands on the door frame to cage her in.

"Don't run," he croaked. "I like the chase."

Tremors rubbed her against him. "So…you want me?"

Do. Not. Answer. "I'm in a state of shock." And awe.

He battled an insane urge to trace his nose along her nape…to inhale the lavender scent of her skin… to taste every inch of her. The heat she projected stroked him, sensitizing already desperate nerve endings.

The mask of humanity he'd managed to don before reentering society began to chip.

Off-kilter, he backed away from her. She remained in place, clutching the lapels of her coat.

"Look at me," Daniel commanded softly.

After an eternity-long hesitation, she turned. Her gaze remained on his feet. Which was probably a good thing. Those shamrock eyes might have been his undoing.

"Why me, Dorothea?" She'd shown no interest in him before. "Why now?"

She chewed on her bottom lip and said, "Right now I don't really know. You talk too much."

Most people complained he didn't talk enough. But then, Dorothea wasn't here to get to know him. And he wasn't upset about that—really. He hadn't wanted to get to know any of his recent dates.

"You didn't answer my questions," he said.

"So?" The coat gaped just enough to reveal a swell of delectable cleavage as she shifted from one foot to the other. "Are we going to do this or not?"

Yes!

No! Momentary pleasure, lifelong complications.
"I—"

"Oh my gosh. You actually hesitated," she squeaked. "There's a naked girl right in front of you, and you have to think about sleeping with her."

"You aren't my usual type." A Strawberry Valley girl equaled marriage. No ifs, ands or buts about it. The only other option was hurting his dad, so it wasn't an option at all.

She flinched, clearly misunderstanding him.

"I prefer city girls, the ones I have to chase," he added. Which only made her flinch again.

Okay, she hadn't short-circuited his brain; she'd liquefied it. Those curves…

Tears welled in her eyes, clinging to her wealth of black lashes—gutting him. When Harlow Glass had tortured Dorothea in the school hallways, her cheeks had burned bright red but her eyes had remained dry.

I hurt her worse than a bully.

"Dorothea," he said, stepping toward her.

"No!" She held out her arm to ward him off. "I'm not stick thin or sophisticated. I'm too easy, and you're not into pity screwing. Trust me, I get it." She spun once more, tore open the door and rushed into the hall.

This time, he let her go. His senses devolved into hunt mode, as he'd expected, the compulsion to go after her nearly overwhelming him. *Resist!*

What if, when he caught her—and he *would*—he didn't carry her back to his room but took what she'd offered, wherever they happened to be?

Biting his tongue until he tasted blood, he kicked the door shut.

Silence greeted him. He waited for the past to re-surface, but thoughts of Dorothea drowned out the screams. Her little pink nipples had puckered in the cold, eager for his mouth. A dark thatch of curls had shielded the portal to paradise. Her legs had been toned but soft, long enough to wrap around him and strong enough to hold on to him until the end of the ride.

Excitement lingered, growing more powerful by the second, and curiosity held him in a vise grip. The Dorothea he knew would never show up at a man's door naked, requesting sex.

Maybe he didn't actually know her. Maybe he should learn more about her. The more he learned, the less intrigued he'd be. He could forget this night had ever happened.

He snatched his cell from the nightstand and dialed Jude, LPH's tech expert.

Jude answered after the first ring, proving he hadn't been sleeping, either. "What?"

Good ole Jude. His friend had no tolerance for bull, or pleasantries. "Brusque" had become his only setting. And Daniel understood. Jude had lost the bottom half of his left leg in battle. A major blow, no doubt about it. But the worst was yet to come. During his recovery, his wife and twin daughters were killed by a drunk driver.

The loss of his leg had devastated him. The loss of his family had changed him. He no longer laughed or smiled; he was like Daniel, only much worse.

"Do me a favor and find out everything you can about Dorothea Mathis. She's a Strawberry Valley resident. Works at the Strawberry Inn."

The faint *click-clack* of typing registered, as if the guy had already been seated in front of his wall of computers. "Who's the client, and how soon does he—she?—want the report?"

"I'm the client, and I'd like the report ASAP."

The typing stopped. "So this is personal," Jude said with no inflection of emotion. "That's new."

"Extenuating circumstances," he muttered.

"She do you wrong?"

I'm not stick thin or sophisticated. I'm too easy, and you're not into pity screwing. Trust me, I get it.

"The opposite," he said.

Another pause. "Do you want to know the names of the men she's slept with? Or just a list of any criminal acts she might have committed?"

He snorted. "If she's gotten a parking ticket, I'll be shocked."

"So she's a good girl."

"I don't know what she is," he admitted. Those corkscrew curls...pure innocence. Those heart-shaped lips...pure decadence. Those soft curves... *mine, all mine.*

"Tell Brock this is a hands-off situation," he said before the words had time to process.

What the hell was wrong with him?

Brock was the privileged rich boy who'd grown up ignored by his parents. He was covered in tats and piercings and tended to avoid girls who reminded him of the debutantes he'd been expected to marry. He preferred the wild ones...those willing to proposition a man.

"Warning received," Jude said. "Dorothea Mathis belongs to you."

He ground his teeth in irritation. "You are seriously irritating, you know that?"

"Yes, and that's one of my better qualities."

"Just get me the details." Those lips…those curves… "And make it fast."

CAN'T HARDLY BREATHE—available soon from Gena Showalter and HQN Books!

COMING NEXT MONTH FROM

HARLEQUIN
Desire

Available October 3, 2017

Get 2 Free Books,
Plus 2 Free Gifts—
just for trying the Reader Service!

HARLEQUIN *Desire*

THE RANCHER'S CINDERELLA BRIDE
SARA ORWIG

LITTLE SECRET: RED HOT SCANDAL
CAT SCHIELD

This was a hell of a time to feel arousal tighten his body.

Dani looked better than any woman should while negotiating the purchase of infant necessities during the beginnings of a blizzard with her brain-dead boss and an unknown baby.

Her body was curvy and intensely feminine. The clothing she wore to work was always appropriate, but even so, Nathaniel had found himself wondering if Dani was as prim and proper as her office persona would suggest.

Her wide-set blue eyes and high cheekbones reminded him of a princess he remembered from a childhood storybook. The princess's hair was blond. Dani's was more of a streaky caramel. She'd worn it up today in a sexy knot, presumably because of the Christmas party.

While he stood in line, mute, Dani fussed over the contents of the cart. "If the baby wakes up," she said, "I'll hold her. It will be fine."

In that moment, Nathaniel realized he relied on her far more than he knew and for a variety of complex reasons he was loath to analyze.

Clearing his throat, he fished out his wallet and handed the cashier his credit card. Then their luck ran out. The baby woke up and her screams threatened to peel paint off the walls.

Dani's smile faltered, but she unfastened the straps of the carrier and lifted the baby out carefully. "I'm so sorry, sweetheart. Do you have a wet diaper? Let's take care of that."

The clerk pointed out a unisex bathroom, complete with changing station. The tiny room was little bigger than a closet. They both pressed inside.

They were so close he could smell the faint, tantalizing scent of her perfume.

Was it weird that being this close to Dani turned him on? Her warmth, her femininity. Hell, even the competent way she handled the baby made him want her.

That was the problem with blurring the lines between business and his personal life.

Don't miss
BILLIONAIRE BOSS, HOLIDAY BABY
by USA TODAY *bestselling author Janice Maynard,*
available October 2017 wherever
Harlequin® Desire books and ebooks are sold.

www.Harlequin.com

Copyright © 2017 by Janice Maynard

HDEXP092017

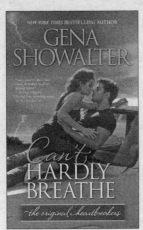

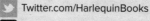
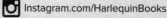
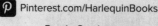
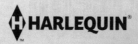

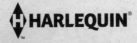